Ava,

Fire & Ice:

The Elementals

Book One

Erin Forbes

By Erin Forbes

Fire & Ice: The Elementals

Copyright © 2016 by Erin Forbes

Cover Design Copyright © 2018 by Jennifer Zemanek/
Seedlings Design Studio

www.fireandicebookseries.com

Third paperback edition 2018

ISBN-13: 978-0-9997719-2-1

Fire & Ice:

The Elementals

Book One

By Erin Forbes

For my parents,
who have always supported my wild
and fantastic dreams.

The Academy for Gifted Youth

Students

Alice Hanley ~ a lion-hearted girl with fire in her veins and flames in her heart

Emery Hanley ~ a pale-faced girl with icy blue eyes and water in the palm of her hand

Ariadne Moss ~ her laughter brings us a gentle breeze

Juniper Stone ~ a tall and wild-haired girl whose gift is just as natural as her name

Ronan O'Reilly ~ a freckle-faced boy with an unbreakable habit of causing things to levitate

Kade O'Reilly ~ feathered friend to our heroine

Violet Holloway ~ a peculiar girl with lavender hair and eyes that change color with her own emotions

Holland Shepard ~ a proper young girl with the Gift of giving color to even the dullest of objects

Grayson Fields ~ a golden-haired boy with light in his hands

Sage Pine ~ wolf-girl

Hugo Stone ~ brother of Juniper Stone

Avery Russell

Bentley Nolan

Staff

Zara Hawthorne ~ Headmistress of the Academy

Professor Georgina Iris

Professor Eleanora O'Connor

Sir Theodore Barrington

Ms. Ruby Lane

Ms. Augusta Emerson

Mr. Oliver O' Reilly

Professor Blakely Biddle

The Guardians of Aisling

Emerson ~ a burly Irish wolfhound
with shimmering golden eyes

Lachlan ~ the finest archer in all of Aisling

Those who dwell in Aisling...

Willoughby ~ an indecisive old troll who
lives deep within the White Birch Forest

The Droplet Faeries ~ a species of tiny
faeries who carry water droplets atop
their heads and build villages out of the
flowers that they tend

The Creatures of the Night Oak Forest
~ invisible to the eye, but not to the mind

Historical Figures of the Realm

Silas Casper ~ founder of The Academy
for Gifted Youth

Wolfgang Gregory ~ responsible for the
curse upon the Night Oak Forest

"The watering can is empty, Emery," said Mother, attempting to avoid my question. "Would you care to refill it for me?"

"Please answer me," I pleaded with her.

"I think it would be better if we spoke about this matter with your father," she responded, before picking up the watering can.

"Tell him to come down here!" Emery and I spoke in unison.

Our mother sighed before closing her brown eyes. They were almost identical to mine; however, behind them was a very different Gift. Our mother could speak to others with nothing more than her thoughts. Even when she was miles away from home, she always managed to step into the mind of her red-haired daughter.

"Your father is coming," she said as she opened her eyes.

After a long moment, our father appeared at the door of the house. A sorrowful expression was settled in the crease between his brows. As we made our way out of the garden, the tall man crossed the expanse of grass. I was beginning to anticipate the news that our parents were destined to share.

"We have something to tell both of you," our father announced as we sat down in the grass. In his hands, he held a small wooden box. A key protruded from its lock, and the opening rested slightly ajar.

"We haven't been entirely honest with the two of you," our mother added.

"Did something happen?" I questioned, noticing the tears that stained her cheeks.

"Your grandmother has passed away," Father murmured, allowing his gaze to drop with his broken spirit.

"A young man was here, early this morning, as a messenger from the realm of Aisling. He gave us the news," our mother explained. "He brought a gift that your grandmother promised to share with both of you."

My mother's strawberry-blonde hair danced gently in the autumn breeze. After pulling up the latch on the tiny wooden box, she placed it gently on the grass. It contained a note and an old cloth bag. The woman's eyes hid the same look of uncertainty that I had seen in those of my sister.

"Your Gifts are very important," our mother told us. "They are anything but ordinary, even for the extraordinary."

CHAPTER ONE

I woke early that morning with glittering eyes as the dawn light danced across my bedroom floor. My twin sister was standing on the other side of the room. Her wavy blonde hair had already been tied back into a perfect french braid. She stood quietly at her bedside, packing her suitcase with an abundance of clothes and heavy-looking books. Emery glanced over her shoulder and seemed almost surprised to see me awake. I stared at her in confusion before my stomach lurched with the sudden realization of what day it was.

"I didn't expect you to be up already," Emery laughed.

"I may as well have been up all night," I groaned before dropping my head back into the comfort of my pillow.

As my sister smirked, I caught sight of the childish laughter she was hiding behind her pale eyes. Emery knew I had been dreading this day, and I knew she had been looking forward to it.

"I don't think this situation is as terrible as you have made it out to be," my sister murmured, attempting to console me.

"How would you know, Emery?" I responded before standing up and walking toward my wardrobe.

"We are talking about the Academy," she responded. "Both our parents and our grandparents have attended the school. Why are you so nervous?"

I thought about this question for a moment and realized I was not entirely sure of an answer. Truthfully, I wasn't quite sure of anything at the moment. A knot was beginning to form in my chest, protecting my heart from the moments that were destined to unfold.

Perhaps it was time for me to explain.

My family is far from average. I suppose one might believe magic runs through our veins. However, many people would be fooled by such a statement, for magic is not as it has been told. It is not like in the fairy tales, where there are evil witches, dragons, and princesses with hair long enough to grow down the side of a tower. In my world, magic is more like a Gift.

There are places where magic is hidden from the average eye, and there are people who refuse to see it. Despite this truth, the faint sparks linger in every shadowed corner of the world. Although it often takes the form of a flickering ember, magic can be found in the heart of every individual.

Three years had passed since the day I discovered my Gift, although I had not grown much fonder of it. A fire had always been so much easier for me to start than it was for me to extinguish.

Glancing back over my shoulder, I noticed Emery was watching me with a careful expression. Her cerulean eyes were flooded with uncertainty, and I knew she was trying to read me. My sister always knew when something was wrong; however, there were moments when I wished she did not. I attempted to block out her gaze by keeping myself occupied. My emotions were too complicated for her to understand.

I opened the door to my wardrobe with haste, only to realize every shelf was abandoned. After rolling my eyes, I pulled a suitcase out from under my bed and fiddled through the stacks of clothing. The majority of my wardrobe was useless in the realm of Aisling, as the popular attire resembled that of medieval ages.

We were leaving for our very first year at the Academy for Gifted Youth, which is a highly respected boarding school within the realm of Aisling. The ancient school was founded nearly a thousand years ago, and it was created for the children of the Gifted society. Despite my dream of visiting the realm of Aisling, my spirit was never fond of change.

Before the age of thirteen, my life was practically ordinary. My youth did not contain a noticeable trace of magic, as I did not believe in the existence of such a thing. The fantasy of fairies and dragons was never a phase in my childhood. Even so, this strange reality eventually came crashing down on both of the Hanley sisters, as our parents attempted to explain that every fickle fable was real.

My family originated in the realm of Aisling, and my parents moved to the ordinary world during my infancy. I did not remember any of this, and my sister and I knew nothing about our true origin before the day of our thirteenth birthday.

That was when everything had changed.

Our parents began to homeschool us after we found out about our Gifts. This idea was brilliant in my opinion. I never had to worry about the occasional ball of fire that dared to burst from the palm of my hand, or the fact that my hair would quite literally go up in flames at the sight of a complicated math problem.

Many of my friends questioned the reason for my departure, and I never found a proper explanation for the matter. The best of my former classmates attempted to reach the Hanley residence by telephone, but my father eventually ran out of excuses for my busy schedule. The majority of old classmates had quit contact after that moment; however, a few of them occasionally sent a letter that was destined to collect dust behind my desk. This may seem a bit harsh, but the topic of my departure was never easy to avoid. The letters eventually stopped, as my friends began to assume I had moved to an address they would never know.

Emery and I became closer in those three years. We had always been there for each other as sisters, but now the two of us were practically inseparable. There were times when I believed she knew me better than anyone in the world.

I sighed with exasperation as I tumbled onto my back, examining the constellations of glow-in-the-dark stars that were scattered across the ceiling. I was not surprised to learn that my sister was happy about the idea of leaving home. We had always been complete opposites.

CHAPTER TWO

I walked down the hallway and into the kitchen, where my mother was flipping pancakes on the stove. A thin layer of steam was beginning to cloud the window above the sink. The fresh scent of berries floated through the air. My father had prepared the table for breakfast. This seemed quite peculiar, as the sun had just barely risen. Nevertheless, I pulled out a chair and sat down at the smooth oak table.

Emery walked in a few moments later, dropping her suitcase neatly beside the door. I had packed several days in advance. I believed this action would help me forget about leaving; however, the strategy had failed.

After a few minutes, our mother placed a plate of blueberry pancakes on the island counter. She topped it off with a glass cover and gestured to the front door. Emery sighed as though she were suddenly out of energy. Despite a moment of complaining, I managed to pull my sister in the direction of the door. We laced up our paddock boots before rushing out into the cold morning air.

The misty morning dew soaked the foot of our boots as we jogged through the field. A faint trace of birdsong floated through the air, following us through the barn doors. Four giant heads peeked out of their stalls and whinnied a greeting. My sister hurried over to her horse, Wellington, and slid his halter over his huge gray face. I unlocked the bottom half of the Dutch door that led to my horse's stall. The gentle creature stood beside the entrance, tossing her head with impatience. My right hand ran over her gleaming chestnut coat. As I secured her halter, she poked at the carrot in my jacket pocket.

Felicity was a tall and well-muscled quarter horse mare with three socks and a heart for jumping. Wellington was a big-boned thoroughbred gelding, who would gladly take part in anything you threw his way. Despite their differences, the two horses were the most loyal of companions.

As we reached the end of the path that ran down the foggy hillside, I pushed open the paddock gate and led my horse inside. I gave the chestnut mare one last stroke on the neck before leaving her to graze.

As I followed Emery up the trail, a quiet sadness overwhelmed my spirit. A terrible realization was beginning to dawn on me; in just a few hours, I would no longer have this experience in my daily life. I was destined to live at the boarding school until winter break. My resentment for the idea of leaving seemed to grow with this thought, but I was reminded I did not have any other choice.

A vast blue and pink horizon spread out as we walked back to the barn. The dew-covered hillside was beginning to grow a little brighter, as the sun rose steadily behind the trees. The distant melody of a songbird flowed like a whisper through the morning air. I was going to miss this place more than anyone would ever know.

"If we want to have any hope of arriving before the portal opens, we will need to leave the house before eight o'clock," my father commented as we stumbled through the kitchen door.

I nodded hastily in response as we joined our parents for breakfast. It was not long before I found myself in the middle of a lecture, while the rest of my family carried on conversation about the fantastic Academy for Gifted Youth. I chugged down my glass of orange juice in an attempt to hide my agitation. My emotions revealed as a spark ignited at my fingertips and set one of the napkins on fire. I stared at the burning cloth in silence before whisking my hand over the flames. Unfortunately, it was too late for me, as a stream of water came bursting from the direction of my twin sister. My long red hair was instantly drenched.

Emery's eyes rounded like two bright moons, while a roar of laughter escaped from our father. The embarrassment was overwhelming; my entire family knew I was unable to control my Gift. I snatched the last bite of my blueberry pancake and hurried up the stairwell. There was exactly one hour before we needed to leave, although it seemed no longer than a moment.

I sat on my bed for several minutes, taking in the sweet scent of my favorite candle and staring at my reflection in the vanity mirror. The bedroom was nearly empty, for almost everything had been packed into my suitcases. I almost forgot something of great importance.

I pulled out a tiny wooden box that was hidden beneath the nightstand. It contained a necklace with a glass vial pendant, which I had received from my grandmother on my thirteenth birthday. The gift had arrived with a note, which instructed me not to open the bottle until I reached the age of sixteen.

Any average thirteen-year-old would probably just shrug and open the necklace right away; however, I was not the average thirteen-year-old. The necklace was hidden under my nightstand ever since. I was not going to be home for my sixteenth birthday, as it fell on the final hours of October. Thus, the piece of jewelry was finally removed from the case. I gently clasped the chain around my neck and tucked the vial into the collar of my shirt. The little wooden box was abandoned in the mess that was scattered beside my duffle bag.

CHAPTER THREE

As I sat beside my sister in the back of our father's blue pickup truck, the series of ordinary moments began to feel surreal. Emery's pale fingers tapped gently on the car window, creating streaks of ice across the glass. The lovely artwork quickly melted in the late summer heat. My eyes were fixed on the old farmhouse that stood beyond the car door. I was attempting to inscribe every inch of our home throughout my memory.

The car ride was several hours long, and we had nothing to entertain us but the music in our ears and the flames that danced across my fingertips. We passed through a countless number of deserted mountain towns and tiny village hamlets. The road was eventually reduced to the elements of dirt and gravel. I wondered if

14

it were possible that another journey ever felt so long; however, a part of me did not wish for the trip to end.

We eventually came to a small stone bridge that was settled over a sun-dappled stream, which rested deep in the unbounded forest. My father parked the truck in the grass before we each stepped out and unloaded our luggage.

Mom placed her arm gently around my shoulders and took the extra duffle from my hand. The morning mist had created a layer of dew upon the meadow grass. Streaks of sunlight were beginning to steal the precious droplets. The far side of the stream was dense with fog.

"Where are we?" Emery whispered.

This was not where I had expected to find a portal to another realm. There was not a house in sight. Nevertheless, between the babbling brook that flowed beneath the cobblestone bridge and the whistle of song-birds that hung in the air, something about the forgotten place seemed magical.

"This is Miller's Bridge," our father spoke, gesturing for us to follow him.

As we made our way around a blossoming tree, we discovered a small group of people gathered near the edge of the water. Most of them appeared to be parents and children; however, an unusual old lady stood in the center of the group. Her patterned skirt dragged along the mossy earth, while a pair of foggy, round spectacles balanced on the tip of her nose. Her hair was a long and wispy gray, and she carried a crooked wood cane.

"Has everyone arrived?" the old woman asked as we made our way closer.

My eyes scanned slowly through the people around me, as if I would recognize at least one of the unfamiliar faces. My eyes caught on a boy who stood beside the water. His freckled face seemed slightly recognizable, although I was sure I had never seen him before.

My father tipped his baseball cap to the peculiar man who stood a few feet away. He was dressed in a brightly colored tweed jacket, and his right eye was an entirely different shade than his left. The strange man waved gleefully toward my father, indicating the years of a longtime friendship.

A lavender-haired girl stood beside the man. I watched her for a long moment, eventually realizing that her eyes seemed to resemble the changing colors of a kaleidoscope. It was obvious she was the strange man's daughter.

"Who are they?" I whispered to my father.

"That would be Sir Emerson Holloway and his daughter, Violet," he responded. "The two of us were great friends when we were your age. We met at the Academy for Gifted Youth."

My parents had never bothered to introduce their children to other members of the Gifted society. Despite the occasional letter that arrived from an unusual address, the normality of my childhood was protected. As a matter of tradition, the Academy refused to accept students with less than three years of experience with their Gift. For many people, the years provided enough time to understand their power.

I was not so fortunate.

This matter was abruptly shoved to the back of my mind, as the elderly woman gestured in our direction. After a moment of confusion, Violet Holloway hurried past us. Her lavender hair blew wildly in the wind as she whispered faintly into the old lady's ear. The woman nodded to her in return as the young girl gestured to an ancient rowboat that floated near the edge of the water.

"Violet," the woman gasped. "Where on earth did you find this unsteady contraption?"

"It was in the boathouse on the other side of the stream," Violet responded with a slight cringe.

"Well, I suppose it will have to do," said the elder, shaking her head with disapproval.

"My name is Eleanora O'Connor," she raised her voice to address the entire gathering. "I have been teaching at the Academy for over thirty years. This young lady is Violet Holloway, and she will be opening the portal for us."

Violet nodded and cleared her throat before gesturing for each of us to take our seat in the rowboat. My heart was beginning to pound. As my mother handed over the orange duffle bag, tears began to stream down my cheeks. I didn't want to admit it, but I was terrified. I would soon be surrounded by a world of strangers.

"Listen to me," our father said with a careful smile. "You must have courage."

After receiving a final embrace, my sister and I stepped into the boat with the other children. The youngest was a brown-haired girl, who looked like she was no more than eight years old. The familiar boy sat behind us, accompanied by a girl with strikingly similar features. I assumed they were twins, although they looked more alike than Emery and me.

Violet stood at the front of the boat, allowing it to sway in unwanted directions. She opened her clenched fist to reveal the small amount of dust that was settled in the center of her palm. The golden matter sparkled and shimmered in the early morning light. As Violet blew the powder from her hand, the particles rushed under the bridge, like a stream of water gliding through the air. As soon as the dust reached the surface of the brook, our boat began to follow swiftly in the same direction. The wind swept my long red hair across my eyes, cutting off the majority of my vision. After a long moment, I tucked the strands behind my ears. The watercraft had arrived at an abrupt halt.

My gaze shifted toward Emery, who released a sudden and horrified gasp. Her eyes were staring down at the floorboards, where water was beginning to flow in from an invisible fracture. The cold stream began to soak through our leather boots.

The boat was sinking.

My eyes shot around wildly, but no one else seemed to be concerned. Eleanora sat contently in the front row with Violet at her side as the boat began to sink deeper by the second. I called out with a panicked voice, but no one took notice until we were each no more than a few heads above the stream.

I felt a tap on my shoulder. My eyes met those of the freckle-faced boy. He seemed even more familiar up close, and I found myself forgetting about the idea of drowning as I began to wonder about his identity. My mind was searching for his blue eyes within my memory; however, I only found a piece of them in the ocean and puddles of rainwater. After no more than a moment of eye contact, I realized the teenage boy recognized me as well.

"Hold your breath," he gasped as a strange expression appeared across his face, and his body disappeared into the water below.

Fear began to overwhelm my spirit, although the rising water extinguished every flame that my anxiety generated. Struggling to keep my head above the surface, I noticed Emery was gone. Suddenly, I felt as though someone were trying to drag me deeper. No longer able to keep my head above the rippling tide, I took one last gasp of air before plummeting into the depths of the ice-cold stream. As I dropped, the air in my lungs never seemed to diminish.

After a long moment, I heard a gasp and opened my eyes. We were no longer drowning in the depths of the gelid stream, as we were standing on the steps of an old mossy castle. I glanced around to see the other students standing at my side. The Academy professor was waiting on the footstep of the door. Behind us was a never-ending patchwork of emerald fields.

As Eleanora pulled open the castle doors, my sister glanced at me with an expression that rested somewhere between confusion and delight.

"Welcome to the Academy for Gifted Youth," the professor announced.

CHAPTER FOUR

Upon entering the Academy for the very first time, my heart felt like that of a young child. It seemed as though the matter of my spirit had changed, for my body welcomed every sight with wide and curious eyes. Every worthless expectation of Aisling seemed to dissolve into the back of my mind.

The unbreakable castle walls climbed upward toward breathtaking cathedral ceilings, and an opal chandelier hung steady in the morning light. The iridescent gemstones reflected shades of pink and blue, as the golden sun shone brightly through the castle windows. On the other side of the entrance hall was a large wooden door, similar to the one we had just walked through. It was held open by a pair of short men, who were dressed in very formal attire.

We followed Eleanora across the marble floor and into an enormous dining hall. The room was lined with hundreds of round tables, each covered in light blue linen and beautiful silver dining sets. There were nearly two hundred students seated, while more continued to arrive. All of the people were Gifted with magical talents, and not one was entirely the same.

Eleanora cleared her throat before pointing us to one of the empty tables, and striding away with her wooden cane in hand. I took my seat beside my sister, while the other twins rested across from us. The remainder of the children wandered off to the other side of the dining hall, where the conversation bustled.

Taking a delicate sip from my glass of water, I peered at the hauntingly identical blue eyes that were settled on the other side of the table. Neither of them flinched at the sight of my gaze, and their stare continued for several uncomfortable minutes.

The girl had short and choppy brown hair, which was a few shades lighter than that of her brother. Her nose was turned up slightly, and her cheeks were faintly dotted with freckles. Despite the few differences between the twins, their eyes were the feature that had given them away.

"My name is Ronan O'Reilly," the boy spoke in a slightly awkward tone. "This is my sister, Kade."

"It's a pleasure to meet you," I responded, before taking another sip of my water. "I'm Alice."

"My name is Emery," my sister added wistfully, tapping her fingers on the table.

22

There was another long pause before anyone spoke again. I could feel the gazes watching me as my mind searched for the proper words. I was not made for small talk and lingering conversation.

"What are your Gifts?" Kade asked with a spark of curiosity.

"I have the Gift of the fire element, and Emery has the Gift of the water and ice elements," I responded before gesturing to my silent sister.

Emery had always been a quiet girl. As her twin sister, I knew there were times when she was not fond of this trait. Her gaze radiated kindness, but she was unable to hide expressions of shyness and uncertainty. I knew it would take her several weeks to adjust to this open environment. The precious secret of our Gifts always seemed to be at stake.

"What about you?" I asked the other twins. "What peculiar talents do you possess?"

"Flight," Kade told us quietly.

"You can *fly*?" Emery gasped.

Kade nodded as she unzipped her purple sweatshirt. She moved her arms a bit, revealing the pair of black wings that were held tightly to her back. Her feathers gleamed between the shades of raven-black and purple in the sunlight. As the girl relaxed, her wings softened and hung gently off the back of her chair.

"Something about this realm makes me feel safe," Kade sighed. "I don't feel like I need to hide anymore."

I nodded in agreement, for I knew the emotions that had entered Kade's heart. When we stepped foot in

Aisling, a heavy weight lifted from my shoulders. It was wonderful to be able to discuss our Gifts in public conversation, without a response of horrified stares.

"What about you, Ronan? Can you fly also?" Emery inquired.

"A boy can dream," Ronan responded. "But twins rarely have the same Gift. I have the talent of telekinesis, which is also known as the power to move objects with my mind."

As Ronan spoke, his glass of water began to float from the edge of the table. It rose higher and higher above our heads until Kade finally took notice. Her brother was still oblivious to the situation, but she quickly stood up on her chair and grabbed the delicate glass from the air. Shaking her head with laughter, Kade placed the crystal glass back on the table.

After a few moments, the entire gathering fell silent. I watched as a young woman stood up from her table and walked over to a large, white podium in the center of the room. Her dark brown hair was quite a contrast to her pale skin and striking gaze. She was clothed in a long, flowing dress with a sapphire cloak. Her chin was held high with confidence and poise.

"Welcome to another year at the Academy for Gifted Youth," she greeted us with a slightly accented voice. "My name is Zara Hawthorne, and this will be my fifth year as the headmistress of the Academy."

I was surprised to learn that a young person was in charge of the entire school. It was evident that the majority of the professors were more than a decade older than the headmistress. It was difficult to imagine the responsibilities that came with such a role. Zara's sharp eyes caught on me like a rosebush filled with thorns, and I realized she was much more than capable of her position.

"I remember my first year at the Academy for Gifted Youth." Zara smiled after pulling her gaze away from mine. "It seems like it happened so long ago, but I will never forget the moment when I walked through those giant wooden doors. To be honest with you, I was petrified; however, this castle became home to some of the most extraordinary years of my life."

The hall filled with scattered applause as Professor Hawthorne's eyes searched through the crowd. Her dark brown hair had been pulled back into a very regal braid, which looked suitable on someone with such a royal essence.

"Aisling is a realm that is filled with remarkable people and adventures that hide around every corner," Zara continued. "You will learn lessons here that will stay with you for the rest of your life. However, perhaps most importantly, you will learn that your Gift is part of what makes you individually rare. The courage to embrace such a notion is a Gift within itself."

The room filled with cheers before another woman stood up. Her bright red hair was similar to mine; however, it was much shorter and severely less curly. The sheer monstrosity of her giant and colorful feather coat was the cause of several gasps across the room. The lady's pursed lips were covered in a ghastly shade of plum lipstick. There were times when I prayed that I would never have the audacity to make such a misguided fashion statement.

"Hello, everyone! Many of you know me as Ruby Lane. I'm often a substitute for a few of our classes, but I also manage the dormitory offices." She paused and shuffled through a few papers on the podium. "I'm here to provide the dormitory assignments."

Kade rolled her eyes. There was quite a bit of mumbling amongst the crowd. It was evident that Ms. Lane was not widely admired.

"All girls of the ages eleven and under are assigned to the Pine Hall dormitory on the west side of the castle," Ms. Lane explained as she tapped her fingernails against the wood. "All boys eleven and under will be in the Cardinal Hall dormitory on the third floor. Girls twelve and up will be in Lancaster Hall on the fourth floor, and all boys of the ages twelve and up will be in Bramble Hall, which is located on the north side of the castle."

I looked back at my newfound companions with grave concern. Ronan and Kade had practically doubled over with laughter.

"Your luggage and schedules have already been placed in your rooms," concluded Ruby.

After everyone finished eating, we were told to remain in our seats until our dormitory was called forward. The dining hall flooded with countless voices, as children and teenagers moved between the tables.

"It was a pleasure to meet both of you." Ronan smiled as Bramble Hall was called forward.

After a few moments, my dormitory followed. Kade tucked her wings gently to her back and stepped out of her chair. We quickly blended in with the growing crowd.

The hall was alive with conversation as we followed Ruby Lane to the giant wooden door. As she turned to glance at us, a great expression of dismay settled across the woman's powdered face. She quickly grabbed hold of an odd-looking pendant, which hung around her neck. She placed it gingerly on her purple lips. After a sudden moment of realization, I clapped my hands over my freckled ears, just in time to spare myself from an ear-piercing shriek. All of the girls had fallen silent as they stared in the direction of the door.

"Would each of you *please* line up in an orderly fashion?" Ruby sighed, as though she were already losing her patience.

The group quickly formed into rows of three. I shuffled around for a minute before discovering an empty spot in the lines.

The short-tempered woman held a scroll tightly in her manicured hands. She nodded curtly before releasing the paper, which unrolled until it reached the floor. Ms. Lane adjusted her pink-framed glasses before she continued to read the paper.

"This is a head count. When I announce your name, you must respond with 'here,'" the lady explained, assuming we were clueless.

"Alexandra Whelan?"

"Here!" responded a curly-haired girl, who was standing in the row behind me.

"Kade O'Reilly?"

"I'm here," I heard my friend's voice answer from a bit farther down the line.

"Sage Pine?"

"Present," replied a short-haired girl with unusual golden eyes.

"Alice Hanley?" she finally asked.

"Here," I responded.

"Emery Hanley?" Ms. Lane continued.

"That's me," my sister chimed in.

There were many more students to read off the list before we walked through the dining hall doors. We followed Ms. Lane through the crowded hallways and up the large stairwell. The walls were covered in cobblestone, and medieval tapestries adorned every passageway. I gazed around in wonder as we weaved through the hallways. The castle was dimly lit, despite the lantern Ruby held high. The silver moonlight did not hesitate to shine brightly through the tall windows. It felt like we had gone back in time, for the realm of Aisling was home to medieval traditions, and electricity was not one of them.

We eventually arrived at a tiny wooden door, which I assumed to be the entrance of Lancaster Hall. The door was missing a handle. Ms. Lane glanced back at us before placing her manicured fingers where the doorknob likely would have been. There was an odd clicking sound as the entrance began to creak open.

I glanced at Violet Holloway. She seemed to believe this was all perfectly normal. As the lavender-haired girl tossed a friendly glance in my direction, I remembered she was a second-year student at the Academy for Gifted Youth. The freshmen must have seemed so entertaining in the eyes of the experienced.

Once the door had opened wide, each of us stepped inside the room. Lancaster Hall was quite larger than the size I had expected. In the far corner of the room stood a white staircase, which spiraled up into the shelter of a library loft. A stained-glass window hid between the bookshelves, revealing a beautiful view of the valley meadows.

My gaze drifted toward the little desk that was nestled below the loft. A young woman was seated in the chair, tapping her fingertips swiftly upon the keys of a curious typewriter. A collection of tiny candles floated gently around the room, illuminating each of the shadowed corners.

Ruby Lane cleared her throat, and the typewriter released a sudden dinging sound before the woman glanced up.

"I must apologize, Ruby. I was just finishing another attendance scroll for the headmistress," the writer stammered as she adjusted her wide-rimmed glasses.

"I don't need an explanation, Augusta," snapped Ruby. "These girls are the students of Lancaster Hall. Do with them what you will—I was only assigned to lead them here. This day is far too hectic for you to be wasting my time."

After Ms. Lane hurried out and slammed the door behind her, a cheerful smile spread across the writer's face. A small gap exposed itself between her two front teeth.

"Welcome to Lancaster Hall! It is so wonderful to meet each of you!" She laughed. "My name is Ms. Augusta Emerson, but I prefer to be called by my first name only. I am the dormitory supervisor for Lancaster Hall."

As Augusta stood up from behind the desk, her brown eyes gleamed in the candlelight. Something about her appearance reminded me of a forest elf, as her curly brown hair failed to hide a pair of pointed ears. Even so, Augusta was much taller than any common elf.

"Each of you will be assigned to a four-person bedroom, which you will be staying in until you graduate. No switching is allowed to take place, without permission from the headmistress," Augusta added. "I have placed name signs above each of the doors. Go ahead and find your rooms before getting settled in. Your suitcases and class schedules will already be there."

I glanced over my shoulder at Emery, who shrugged with a smile as we pushed open our bedroom door. The chamber was about half the size of the main dormitory hall. There was a total of four bedframes, which were decorated with golden quilts. In addition to the four wardrobes that stood on the far side of the room, we were provided with the heavy trunks nestled at the end of our beds. A castle window stood tall at the back of the chamber. It revealed a beautiful view of the valley meadows, which reminded me of home.

CHAPTER FIVE

My suitcases were stacked in a neat pile, which had been placed beside the spare bed. The two other girls began to unpack, while my sister rested on the bed across from mine. Her blue eyes wandered the room with an expression of amazement.

After a few minutes, I dragged a heavy suitcase over to my wardrobe. As I unzipped the extra duffle, an explosion of clothing tumbled out of the bag. Despite my calm composure, my mind was racing like the legs of a greyhound. Even the wardrobe was elegant. The sparkling glass handles glittered in the sunlight, and the doors were hand-carved with beautiful and intricate designs. I ran my freckled fingers down the wood, before opening the wardrobe doors. A small collection of wool sweaters was stacked on the shelves above the empty hangers. I pulled out one of the scarlet pieces of fabric, noticing the Academy crest embroidered into the chest. It displayed the head of a golden lion and white unicorn.

After returning the sweater to the dusty closet, I began to unpack my old clothing. It was difficult to find something that would match the typical attire of the Gifted society. My blue jeans and sneakers were useless in the realm of Aisling. A simple white dress and slippers were the only solution.

Emery was still organizing her shoes when something caught my eye. The wardrobe doors were not entirely the same. Glancing back at mine, I noticed the closet was engraved with the wings of a monarch butterfly. A flaming border lined the edge of the red wood, imitating the nature of my elemental Gift. My sister's wardrobe displayed the intricate design of a winter snowflake.

"What's wrong, Alice?" Emery inquired as she glanced up from her suitcase.

"Have you noticed the wardrobe doors?" I responded, running my fingers down the carvings on the wood.

My sister looked at me with an expression of confusion before she stood up to inspect. A layer of fascination masked any trace of her expected suspicion.

"Positively peculiar! I don't have any sort of fancy carving on my wardrobe," said Kade. Glancing over to where her wardrobe stood, I realized that our new friend was right. Despite the wildflowers that had been engraved into the border, her closet was rather dull.

The other girl was starting to unpack some books into her trunk before she glanced over at us. Ariadne seemed like a very quiet person. The short-haired girl reminded me of my twin sister; however, she had not spoken a word since we walked through the door. I was beginning to wonder if she disliked me.

After a moment of contemplation, I walked across the room and examined Ariadne's wardrobe. The design on the door was far from simple. A large oak tree had been carved into the wood, surrounded by the floating foliage of autumn. My amber eyes reviewed the details carefully. It appeared as though the leaves were moving, although the activity was merely an illusion.

My gaze wandered over the endless number of novels piled around Ariadne. It was clear she enjoyed reading. Wondering how she would manage to fit all of her books into a single trunk, I knelt down beside the girl and picked up a heavy volume. I flipped through the first few pages of the old hardcover, eventually realizing it was a copy of my favorite book about the Gifted realm. Ariadne watched me behind curious gray eyes.

"What is your Gift?" I inquired, tucking a strand of ginger hair behind my ear.

"Wind," the girl responded with a faint smile.

"I can see you like to read," I remarked.

Ariadne nodded as she picked up another book and placed it into the trunk. Despite my fickle doubts, she managed to fit all of the novels inside.

I pushed open the big green trunk at the end of my bed. As I organized the small space that dwelled between the wood, time seemed to pass with the pace of a snail. Countless books and art supplies were piled to the brim. When it seemed as though every item had been removed from my duffle bag, a piece of silver metal caught my attention. It was nothing more than a little picture frame, which contained a photo of my family riding our horses on the forest trails. A part of my heart wished to return home for a moment; however, a different piece was beginning to understand the true worth of Aisling.

❧❧❧

After several hours, a quiet knock sounded at the door. The brilliant sunset had faded away from the distant line of trees. Constellations of silver stars were scattered across the velvet sky. A lazy glow of moonlight illuminated the surrounding meadows. I looked up at the old clock that was displayed above the wooden door; the time had passed with swift and silent footsteps.

"Come in," Kade replied as Augusta's head peeked through the doorway.

"I just wanted to let you girls know that everyone must be asleep before ten o'clock," Augusta reminded us. "It would be wise to settle down early tonight, as your classes begin tomorrow morning."

We nodded before Augusta closed the door behind her. The light of our lanterns flickered against the walls, casting shadows across the elegant furniture.

"I'm going to bed," Ariadne muttered. She flicked her wrist, allowing a breeze to snuff the candle on her bedside table.

I glanced over at my fair-haired sister, realizing she had already changed into her nightgown. Emery's pale nose was hidden between the pages of a thick book. The binding was tattered and faded, indicating the many years of love it had received. After a long moment, she glanced up at me with an unreadable expression.

It was not long before everyone else had fallen asleep, and I was the only person awake. I changed into my nightgown and curled up under the bedspread. I knew the other girls were asleep, as no one had objected to Emery's constant snoring. Uncertain darkness lingered in the shadowed corner of the room. With a snap of my fingers, the flame inside of my lantern extinguished into a little puff of smoke. I stared into the eternal darkness of the arched ceiling, while anticipation wandered through my tired mind.

CHAPTER SIX

I must have fallen asleep eventually. It felt like merely a moment before I woke to the morning sunlight leaping through the old castle window. As I wiped the sleep from my eyes, a loud yawn escaped. The sudden sound jolted my sister awake.

"Alice!" Emery scolded me as she sat with her hand upon her chest.

"Oh, calm down! I didn't set the room on fire this time." I laughed before crawling out of my bed and adjusting the quilt.

Ariadne was already dressed and filling her messenger bag with a heavy load of books. We each glanced over at Kade, as she continued to sleep under her blanket.

"Shall we leave her?" Ariadne suggested with the slightest hint of humor in her voice. I was silently surprised by her sudden interest in the conversation, although I shook my head and giggled.

Emery gave me a devious look before sneaking quietly across the hardwood floor. Her plan was not difficult to guess, for she had pulled the very same trick on me. As Emery placed her cold finger on the tip of Kade's nose, the room immediately shook with a massive sneeze. Our new friend awoke with a fright. She blinked with an expression of confusion.

"Why are you waking me up this early?" Kade groaned as she rubbed her frozen nose.

"Well," I responded. "I'm sure you don't want us to leave you. The first class starts in fifteen minutes, and we are all going to be late." I hurried over to my wardrobe and pulled out the scarlet sweater.

"Are you serious?" Kade shrieked, picking up the alarm clock on her bedside table. "I forgot to set my alarm!" She leaped out of bed, throwing blankets into the air.

❧❧❧

We hurried through the hallways and down the towering stairwell. The castle was silent despite the sound of my boots, which tapped quickly against the cold stone floor. A sudden realization had dawned on me—we were late for our very first class. The three of us broke out into a desperate run. By the time we reached the other side of the stone castle, our lesson had started five minutes beforehand.

We barged through the closed door, only to find ourselves interrupting the beginning of a lecture. Our skin was immediately burned with the stares of our classmates. The professor greeted us with a stern and disapproving glare. It was obvious that she was anything but pleased.

"I apologize for our late arrival," I spoke softly.

Our teacher was an elderly woman with silky hair and purple spectacles, which rested low on her crooked nose. She wore a long blue skirt and thick neckerchief, which looked like it had been torn from one of the hallway tapestries. The professor glanced at us before gesturing to the three empty chairs that stood in the back of the classroom.

"What are your names?" she asked before we had a chance to sit down.

"Kade O'Reilly," my friend murmured with a hint of confusion in her voice.

"I know who *you* are," the old woman snapped. "You've been attending this school since you were eleven, Kade. How poor do you think my memory is?"

A wave of giggles spread like wildfire across the classroom. My winged friend took her seat, allowing her cheeks to burn crimson.

"My name is Emery Hanley," my sister announced before sitting down.

The old woman adjusted her purple spectacles before glancing down at her papers. After a moment, she looked up at me with a jaded expression.

"I'm Alice Hanley," I introduced myself before walking through the maze of desks and taking a seat beside my sister.

"Well, you must be the Hanley twins," the professor remarked. "Zara Hawthorne has told me about you."

The entire classroom swiftly flooded with whispers. Nevertheless, as the old professor cleared her throat, the room fell silent. I didn't care much about the opinions of the other Gifted children. My mind was running over the short sentence of the teacher. The headmistress knew my name; perhaps more importantly, she included my name in the topic of her recent conversation.

"Well then, off we go!" the old woman announced before rising from her chair and heading for the door.

As the students stood up and grabbed their bags, the classroom was overwhelmed by the sound of chairs dragging against wood. What was happening? Why were we leaving the classroom when it seemed as though the lesson had just begun? This was not what I had expected. My sister looked back at me with bewilderment as we followed the rest of our class into the hall.

"As we move our lesson into nature, I will give a bit of an introduction for our new students. I would appreciate your full attention," the old woman spoke with a stern expression as she continued to walk down the hall.

"My name is Professor Georgina Iris; however, in this school, you will call me by my first name only. This same principle applies to each and every one of your teachers at the Academy for Gifted Youth," the professor noted as we reached the entrance hall.

The sound of our footsteps was beginning to echo across the marble flooring. Although she was an elderly woman, Georgina Iris walked with an incredibly fast pace. I must have been at least a foot taller than the lady, although my legs rushed to keep up with her quick strides.

"Each of your classes will have a different atmosphere," Georgina continued. "Some of our professors enjoy teaching their students in the castle, while others prefer to work in the outdoors." She stepped over to the towering castle doors before we followed her outside.

"We will be going out to the meadow today," Georgina spoke, as her brown eyes watched us behind cloudy spectacles. "Before the lesson begins, I shall give a brief explanation of the Presentation of the Gifted."

Nobody dared to speak a word as we hurried down the castle steps. We turned onto the path that led toward the open field. Every so often, I glanced around at the other students. A few of their familiar faces had greeted me at the welcome ceremony, and I wondered about the Gifts each of them possessed.

We crossed the path of several little students, who followed in the footsteps of a young and energetic teacher. Two girls dragged behind the group, unable to contain a melody of childish laughter. One of the individuals was shooting colorful puffs of fog into the air. I watched with curiosity as she tossed her arms toward the sky.

"Her name is Holland Shepard."

I jumped at the sound of the voice. Ronan O'Reilly was walking beside my shoulder, grinning at the amusement of my reaction.

"Holland has a bit of an odd talent," Ronan remarked as we stepped into the field. "She can manipulate colors."

"How long has she been here?" I inquired, feeling surprised to encounter such young children.

"About two years," Ronan responded as we came to the center of the meadow.

Georgina gestured for the group to form a circle as we each sat down. It felt good to be outside, with the breeze blowing through my hair and the fresh air filling my lungs. The field seemed to contain a magical essence. My eyes crinkled into a subconscious smile as they soaked in every detail of the magnificent surroundings.

Aisling did not have the landscape that many people might expect of a foreign realm. It was quite similar to our ordinary world, although the meadows held an unexplainable and wild freedom. The only building nearby was the castle that sheltered the Academy for Gifted Youth. If an observant person searched into the distance, they might even catch sight of a small stone village. I wasn't quite sure that cities existed in a realm like Aisling; however, I was beginning to accept this concept.

One could not help but feel as though they were holding hands with Mother Nature, and she had gifted them with the power to see the world through a different pair of eyes. In the faint distance, the meadow grass met a forest of birch trees. Even from where we rested, the group was able to observe the slow and steady dance of the branches.

Once everyone found a suitable place in the grass, the conversation began to diminish. Georgina cleared her throat before speaking. "Today is your first official day at the Academy for Gifted Youth, which means you will be participating in the Presentation of the Gifted."

Immediate whispers and muttering followed this statement. The old woman eventually clapped her hands together, bringing the voices to a sudden silence.

"Many of you may be anxious about this event, but the presentations are quite simple," Georgina told us. "The entire Academy will gather in this field to present the students of the new year. Each of those individuals will receive three minutes to display their Gift in some way or form. Each of you must decide how you will present your power, and I encourage you to be creative."

My heart felt as though it had begun to beat a little faster with the thought of standing in front of the entire school. I did not know how I was supposed to present my elemental Gift. I was not entirely sure I would be able to conjure up an idea in just a few hours.

"If you looked at the back of your schedules given to you upon your arrival, you would have been informed the students have only two classes before the presenta-tions," explained Georgina. "Classes will resume as usual tomorrow morning."

I forgot to glance at the back of my schedule. The expressions of my fellow students suggested an identical situation.

There was a long moment of silence before Ronan tapped me on the shoulder. I suddenly noticed the horrific stares coming from each of my classmates. My anxiety was growing like a weed, and my hair was catching aflame.

Georgina must have eventually taken notice, for she paused her discussion and turned her attention toward my side of the circle. It was evident she was holding back a burst of laughter.

"I suppose we will have to work on that," said Georgina.

"Sorry," I muttered as Emery began to douse my head in water.

CHAPTER SEVEN

The remainder of Georgina's lesson was exceptionally captivating. She told us about her Gift and journey to placement as a teacher at the Academy for Gifted Youth. The elderly woman had the ability to understand any language as though it were her own. The professor told us about the discovery of her Gift. Despite the fact that she had never taken any classes in foreign language, she had extraordinary multilingual abilities. In my opinion, this was extraordinary; after all, it seemed like a very useful talent.

As we walked back to the old castle, my eyes carefully examined the exterior of the stone structure. The tall, mossy walls were reminiscent of the ancient castles in Ireland and Scotland, which my family had visited during the previous summer. Four stone towers stood tall in the distance, suggesting the potential hideaway of a princess.

Once we gathered inside the castle, the professor bid us farewell. The group scattered across the entrance hall, hurrying off to the next classes. As my legs carried me toward the nearby corridor, I retrieved the schedule that was folded in one of my pockets.

"Alice!"

I stopped in my tracks and turned to greet the voices that had called my name. Kade and Ronan hurried through the crowded hallway. A pair of similar smiles illuminated their freckled cheeks. Despite my muddled and confused emotions, the twins did not fail to bestow their happiness on my spirit.

"What is your next class?" Kade asked curiously as her wings swept gracefully behind her.

The Academy for Gifted Youth

Class Schedule
Student Name: Alice Hanley

7:30-8:30 a.m.: Exploring your Gift with
Professor Georgina Iris

8:45-9:45 a.m.: Enchanted Creatures with
Sir Theodore Barrington

10:00-11:00 a.m.: Free Period (studying suggested)

11:30 am-12:15 p.m.: Lunch in Dining Hall

*12:30-1:15 p.m.: Study of Gifts with
Mr. Oliver O'Reilly*

*1:20-2:00 p.m.: Realm History & Exploration with
Professor Blakely Biddle*

*Class time over—please return to the Dining Hall for
dinner at precisely 6:15 p.m.*

As we continued to walk down the hallway, I handed my schedule to the brown-haired girl. Streaks of dark shadows crossed the stone floor, while sunlight streamed through the castle windows. My newfound companions peered over the piece of paper with bright curiosity in their eyes.

"I knew it!" Kade suddenly exclaimed. "Enchanted Creatures is your next class."

"Follow me," Ronan said, before taking a sharp turn down the next hallway.

No more than fifteen minutes later, we were standing in another silent classroom, although there was not a single desk in sight. An old green chalkboard and large stack of books were the only items in the room.

A tall, white-haired man hurried through the open door. Each of the students turned their attention toward the professor, who continued to pile more books in the corner of the room. He eventually noticed our presence and rushed over to the green chalkboard.

47

"Welcome to your second class. My name is Sir Theodore Barrington, and I will be teaching you about the subject of enchanted creatures," the man announced before jotting his name down with a piece of chalk. He gestured for us to take a seat on the floor.

"As many of you know, the vast majority of the creatures in the realm of Aisling do not exist in other worlds. This class was created to teach you precisely about those creatures," Professor Barrington explained. "In time, you will learn this land is home to animals of both beauty and terror. You must understand this class was not created for the faint of heart. Nevertheless, it is essential to learn as much as you can about this subject. I suggest you pay special attention to the details."

Ronan listened with a remarkable expression of interest upon his face. There was a sudden and loud snap that followed this observation. My classmates instantly jolted into a defensive stance. As I whipped my head around, a giant, black-haired figure appeared on the other side of the room. I was unable to identify the species of the creature, as it faced with its back toward us. Each of the students scrambled up from the floor with haste.

After a long moment, the animal turned to meet our anxious gazes. It quickly became apparent that the beast was an enormous black wolf. Each of the students slowly backed up until they stood beside our professor. The wolf merely gazed upon us with uninterested golden eyes; the canine did not display any signs of aggression. If one were to watch with observant eyes, they might even notice the faint expression of amusement hidden behind the creature's smile.

"This is Sage," our teacher told us. "In human form, she is a fourteen-year-old girl. I'm sure you have seen her around the castle. Perhaps, if you are one of the young ladies in Lancaster Hall, she is your roommate."

A collection of delicate whispers swept across the empty floor, colliding in the center of the room. Fearful expressions gradually dwindled in the eyes of rapt teenagers.

"She is not a werewolf." Sir Barrington shook his head, as though he were acquainted with the voices of our thoughts. "Sage is Gifted, just like each of us, although she is studying to become a Guardian of Aisling. She takes several exclusive classes, which the Academy offers by invitation."

"My uncle has the Gift of transformation as well," said the blond boy who stood beside me. "Although, I'm sure he could never be a Guardian. His other form is nothing more than a little rabbit."

"You might be surprised, Grayson." Our teacher smiled. "The Guardians of Aisling accept Gifted people of all different sorts, especially those with the ability to transform."

As he spoke, Professor Barrington reached into the front pocket of his neatly ironed shirt. He retrieved a small compass, which displayed a golden insignia on the cover. I recognized the detailed design, for it was the crest of the Guardians of Aisling. The students stared at the professor with an expression of surprise.

"You are one of the Guardians of Aisling?" Grayson questioned, unable to hide a look of astonishment.

"The Guardians keep the castles and villages safe, and they guard the children of Aisling from harm," said Professor Barrington, ignoring the question. "Even the tiniest of songbirds can find a place among the ranks; however, they must be chosen. Yes, Mr. Nolan?" He pointed toward a boy at the edge of the group.

"How can one tell a Guardian apart from any wild animal that might be wandering through the forest?" The boy lowered his hand, which had been waving wildly in the air. His question addressed the very thought that had been floating through my mind. It would seem very silly to start a conversation with a common hedgehog. They are nothing in comparison to cats, who surely understand the human language.

"Would you care to answer that question?" Our teacher glanced down at the shadowed wolf.

The creature began a low howl. In a matter of sec-onds, it had transformed into a petite girl with curly hair. She appeared to be perfectly ordinary, although her eyes remained a bright hue of gold.

"Almost every Guardian of Aisling can be identi-fied by their golden eyes, but another common trait is the crescent moon birthmark that can be found on the underside of our wrists," Sage explained as she held up her arm.

After a few minutes, our teacher thanked the girl and gestured for her to take her place with the class. I was fascinated with her unusual Gift; however, several students continued to watch the young girl with careful and anxious eyes.

Sir Barrington quickly began another lecture on the various species of poisonous insects and plants that could only be found in Aisling. The topic seemed dull compared to what we had just learned. My focus began to drift.

Eventually, the bell rang, and each of the students piled out of the empty classroom. As I gathered my books and put them into my messenger bag, a hand tapped on my shoulder. Kade was standing behind me. She was accompanied by a group of several teenagers.

"We are all walking down to the meadow for the Presentation of the Gifted," said Kade. "Perhaps you would like to join us."

I nodded and followed her out of the classroom. My heart was pounding loudly in my chest, imitating the steady rhythm of a drum.

"Will you be presenting, too?" I inquired.

"Only first-year students are required to present," Violet Holloway answered.

"Does that mean I'm the only one of us who will be presenting?" I asked.

"It's not like you'll be completely alone," Kade reminded me. "You will have your sister beside you."

"I know plenty of first-year students who are presenting," added Violet, attempting to assure me.

I was hesitant to believe such a statement, as I had not met another first-year student. Nevertheless, the school was relatively large, and my suspicions were likely to be wrong.

"Oh, Alice! Don't be so nervous!" Kade scoffed as we pushed open the large castle doors and hurried down the gravel path.

The manor was teeming with students of all ages, and the path was terribly congested. My eyes searched the crowd for my sister, but she was nowhere to be found. As we reached the edge of the field, five sets of wooden bleachers appeared in the center of the meadow. Almost every seat had been filled—the entire school was here.

I stopped walking. It took a moment for the rest of my friends to realize, although Violet eventually turned around. As she doubled back from the rest of the group, I noticed a glimmer of sympathy in her kaleidoscopic eyes.

"Are you all right, Alice?" Violet asked.

"I can't do this," I whispered.

"You *can* do this," Violet said in a kind voice, which may have been confused for that of an old friend. "I know you are scared, and you have every right to be, for many people are going to be watching you. But you must know that each of us is here to support and embrace your Gift."

I could barely hear her voice my mind was so focused on the echo of my surroundings. Violet pointed me toward a small booth that stood on the other side of the field. A long line of students trailed away from the front, although they were moving forward with swift strides.

"Go check in," Violet instructed me. "Ruby Lane will be at the booth, and she will tell you where to wait for the presentations. I think you should find your twin sister."

I hurried over to my place in the line, while Violet and Kade found a spot in the grandstands. My hands were shaking. I had tried to think of an idea for the presentations, although nothing seemed to be creative enough. I wanted my act to be noteworthy.

Standing up on my toes, I searched the crowd for Emery. She was not too difficult to find in a gathering, for there were few girls with such fair hair. Even so, I did not see her anywhere, and the line was beginning to move along. I allowed panic to ignite an orange ball of flame in my right hand.

CHAPTER EIGHT

Once I reached the entrance booth, Ruby Lane handed me a form to sign. I flipped through the pages until I found my last name. My sister's signature was already written on the paper. I quickly jotted down my name and handed back the peculiar clipboard.

"Thank you very much," said Ruby, before pointing toward the presentation area. "I want you to go through the gate. You must line up with the other students in the middle of the field."

A tall guard stood beside the entrance. His face was dark and expressionless. As he held open the gate, however, I was sure I spotted an expression of sympathy in his golden eyes.

"Thanks," I murmured.

My skin crawled as I hurried across the open field. The eyes of countless students and professors seemed to be glaring at my shaking hands. A trail of burnt grass was left in my wake. The group of new students provided a shelter from the judgmental stares.

I could have sworn I heard someone calling my name. Glancing over to the right side of the gathering, my eyes caught sight of Emery. My sister was standing a few feet away. She waved and began to switch places with the other students until she stood by my side. Her gaze was bright with excitement.

"I must have searched the entire castle for you! Did you enjoy the last class?" Emery asked, pulling her long blonde hair back into a ponytail.

"It was fascinating." I nodded before staring into the crowd.

Violet, Kade, and Ronan were seated at the top of the middle grandstand. Their faces beamed with laughter as they waved at us.

"I've been talking to Ariadne Moss," said Emery. "She was in my last class today, and we were assigned as partners for the assignment. Believe it or not, the girl has quite the attitude."

"Is that so?" I inquired, glancing at her with an expression of surprise.

"She must have argued with the history teacher for over half an hour!" exclaimed Emery, rolling her eyes.

A sudden and thunderous explosion erupted from behind us. We whipped our heads around to see the headmistress standing on the stage. An electric shriek filled the air as Ruby Lane attempted to adjust the antique microphone that stood in front of the professor. After a long moment, Zara waved her hand, gesturing for Ruby to take a seat.

"Welcome to the Presentation of the Gifted," Zara's proper voice bellowed through the microphone as the crowd erupted into cheers. "I'm very pleased to announce that we have a wealth of talented first-year students."

I glanced at Emery, and she smiled in return. My sister's face had grown unusually pale, and her eyes were even wider than normal. I realized the event was just beginning to settle in her mind.

"The first student to present will be Avery Russell," Zara continued, gently unrolling a scroll that had been placed on top of the podium.

As I looked down the line of children, a young girl stepped forward. Her blonde hair fell just beneath her shoulders, and her eyes were a striking shade of emerald green.

"I shall kindly ask for each of the remaining first-year students to take a seat in front of the stage," Zara announced as she gestured to the line of tree stumps that rested just below the stage.

We each took our seats, leaving the girl in the center of the field. I watched in surprise as she sat down in the grass. After a brief moment, she began to levitate above the meadow. I wondered if she would float away. Nevertheless, as she tilted her head to the side, Avery's entire body flipped upside down in the air. Her Gift reminded me of a circus acrobat, although she was not held in the air by ribbons or an invisible string.

As her long arms reached toward the grass, the girl began to lower herself to the position of a handstand. Her hair dangled gently toward the ground. She eventually stood back on her feet, and the crowd exploded into cheers. As the young girl returned to her seat, my mind continued to search for a unique idea.

"Avery Russell is twelve years old, and she is Gifted with the power of levitation," Zara announced as she stepped back up to the podium. "Avery is the only Gifted individual in her family."

I wondered what it would be like to be the only Gifted person in the Hanley clan. It seemed like such a life would be lonely. Despite our extraordinary lives, my Gifted family was a treasure.

"Hugo Stone will be the next child to present his Gift," the headmistress told us.

I glanced around in search of the boy, but none of the students stood up from their seat. Out of the corner of my eye, I spotted a figure in the center of the field. Turning their heads, each of the students looked at the boy in confusion. My breath released with the satisfaction of knowing I was not the only one who had seen him appear out of thin air.

"Hugo is one of the youngest students at the Academy for Gifted Youth. Many of you probably know his sister, Juniper Stone, who is currently visiting one of the isles off the coast of Aisling," the headmistress spoke as the young boy continued to disappear and reappear across the field. "Hugo has the remarkable Gift of making himself invisible to the human eye for short periods of time. Such a power may appear similar to teleportation, although the experience is entirely different."

As Hugo returned to his seat, the teachers and children laughed. Before I had a moment to collect my thoughts, my sister was standing up. We barely made eye contact before she hurried into the center of the field.

"At the age of thirteen, Emery Hanley discovered that she has been Gifted with the water element. She can control and manipulate both water and ice, and she possesses extraordinary talent for someone with so little training," Zara announced before giving my sister the signal to begin.

Suddenly, a rolling ball of water appeared in the palm of Emery's hand. As she threw it toward the sky, the water began to roll out in waves. I heard the gasps of the students beside me. The sparkling water tossed around my sister, as though she were the center of a raging whirlpool. Her long hair blew wildly in the wind, and she did nothing more than stomp her foot to the ground as the waves froze into a solid sculpture.

Once again, the audience roared with excitement. My gaze wandered the crowd, analyzing the various expressions of wonder and awe. Emery eventually took her seat beside me, and it was not long before the headmistress called my name. As I stood up and walked into the center of the field, it felt like a knot had formed in my stomach. I told myself not to look at the audience, but my gaze instinctively darted up to greet them.

"Alice Hanley has the extraordinary Gift of the fire element," Zara told the crowd. "Despite the difference in appearance, she is the twin sister of Emery Hanley."

As Zara gestured for me to begin, I turned toward the frozen waves that my sister had created. Cold water droplets dripped gently from the ice, as the late summer heat shone down from the sky. Closing my eyes, I focused on the waves. Heat radiated off my outstretched palms, as if I was warming them beside a winter fire. The water droplets began to stream from my sister's creation, until the ice was nothing more than a puddle in the meadow grass. I heard a few gasps and whispers, but the reaction did not satisfy my expectations. I wanted to give the crowd something to remember.

As my gaze wandered the field, an amusing idea entered my imagination. Glancing over my shoulder, I dared to look back at Emery's suspicious mien. She knew my thoughts before I had even known them myself. I gave her a humorous grin before both of my hands were set ablaze.

The crowd stood up in shock. My eyes searched through the audience as a smile spread wide across my face. I reached behind me and set my ginger hair on fire. A few people screamed, but my sister laughed with the careless attitude of a child. My mind recalled the first time this situation had occurred.

I had been reading in the dim light of my flames, when a piece of my red mane dipped into the fire. My entire head was crowned in flames. Despite the horrified expressions of my parents, the accident quickly turned into a habit and entertaining game. Due to the traits of my Gift, my skin was unable to burn in the heat.

I gave a small curtsy before walking back to my seat, where my sister began to extinguish the flames. The crowd was still cheering by the time the next student made their way into the field. As my eyes wandered through the faces in the crowd, Professor Georgina Iris watched me with an approving smile.

After the presentations ended, the crowd began to dissipate. I pushed my way through the scattered clusters of people, leading my sister through the gathering. It was not long before my eyes caught sight of Violet, as her purple hair stood out in the crowd. She was standing at the bottom of the grandstand, accompanied by Kade and Ronan.

"Oh, Alice!" Kade exclaimed. "That was brilliant!"

"You were both incredible," Ronan added.

"You made our first-year presentations look like nothing in comparison to your own!" Violet threw her head back with laughter as we began to walk toward the castle.

"Shall we go to the dining hall for lunch?" Violet suggested as she fiddled with the silver ribbon around her neck.

We trotted up the old castle steps and swung open the heavy door. As my stomach released a sudden rumble, I was reminded of the fact I had missed breakfast.

"Oh, yes! I'm starving," Ronan complained as we hurried through the crowded entranceway.

Our shoes clapped loudly on the smooth stone flooring. Not long after we entered the dining hall, a group of young students rushed in my direction. Their eyes were wide with curiosity.

"Does the fire burn?" questioned a girl with curly hair and caramel skin.

"Have you ever set something on fire by accident?" asked the boy who stood beside her.

I looked down at the children with an expression of uncertainty. Their eyes sparkled with wonder and admiration. Their interest in my Gift was flustering, although my body relaxed with the knowledge that the young people did not see me as a danger. I had grown used to the idea of locking my talent in an invisible box. This admiration took me by surprise.

As I felt a hand tap on my shoulder, my eyes turned to see Ronan standing quietly by my side. His gentle touch had caused me to jump. The boy snorted with laughter before his freckled face was overcome with a serious expression.

"I'm sure Alice will have time to answer your questions later," Ronan spoke to the children, hinting for them to leave me alone.

They looked up at the older boy with expressions of annoyance written firmly across their adolescent faces. For a long moment, I wondered if they would listen. The children turned away and hurried back to their seats at a small table, which erupted with the high-pitched giggles of younger students.

"Thank you for your assistance," I murmured.

"No problem," Ronan laughed. "It seems you are the latest school celebrity."

We made our way through the crowd of students and over to the table where our friends were seated. Emery gave me an awkward smile before I claimed an empty chair. Paying no attention to her childish expressions, I poured a cup of tea.

We each ate a bowl of oatmeal, which, for some reason, did not taste quite like the kind from home. The tables were lined with several plates of warm toast and tiny bowls of sweet-smelling jam. The glorious scent left me to reminisce about Saturday morning breakfast with my father.

The centerpiece was surrounded by a wide variety of unfamiliar fruits and berries. Ronan picked up one of the pieces that resembled a peach. As the teenage boy took a bite, the inside revealed a vibrant shade of blue. His lips pursed with a reaction to the sour taste.

Despite my homesickness, I tried to make the best of the experience. Small conversations were beginning to flow with ease. Each of my new friends spoke with a glimmer in their eyes, which promised to remain for countless years. It was too early for me to make any allegations about what the future might hold, but my heart hoped for the best. My classmates were interested in every word that leaped from their peers, and they embraced my Gift with marvelous encouragement. I was eager to explore the realm of Aisling, and my new companions offered to be my guide.

"That reminds me," Emery exclaimed after taking another bite of her oatmeal. "Georgina told everyone in the class to pick up two boxes of fireleaf and petalstone for an upcoming project."

"Perfect! I can take both of you on a tour of the old village," Violet offered. "You'll be able to find some petalstone at the Moss Shop, although fireleaf is quite expensive. It would probably be best to forage it in the White Birch Forest. I think I know just the spot where we would be able to find it."

"That sounds great," I responded.

After we finished eating lunch, many of the students wandered off to study in the library. Such an idea was wise enough, but it did not provide my spirit with the fuel of adventure. I stood on the edge of the castle steps, gazing out at the vast landscape that rested before me. Four outlandish towers stood on the castle grounds. Other students had mentioned the structures in conversation, only to say the doors were locked and there was no sense in trying to open them. So many unexplainable secrets. After a quick glance behind me, I continued to walk down the gravel path that led toward the courtyard.

The courtyard was a large garden surrounded by old stone walls, which were covered in an assortment of flowering vines. I stopped myself before allowing my hands to brush against their leaves. Sir Barrington's lecture had reminded me to be conscious of the possible dangers in the poisonous plants of the realm.

The garden was bursting with color. I was sure my body had stepped through an entrance to the Victorian era. In the center of the courtyard was a fountain of water, which flowed out of thin air. Along the sides of the path were the most brilliant flowers I had ever seen. I allowed my wonder to guide my feet down the cobblestone path. As the sunset welcomed the first stars of the night, I came to a halt at the sight of something unusual.

On the far side of the courtyard stood a stone bench, where a figure was seated with her back toward me. I immediately recognized the mousy brown hair of Ariadne Moss.

"Hello, Alice," she spoke as I approached her.

I took a seat on the bench. Silence lingered between us for several moments. Tears glistened like fresh rain upon Ariadne's face. Her eyes were a cloudy shade of gray, and her nose was dotted with faded freckles. A small bundle of fur rested gently in the crook of her elbow.

"Ariadne, are you okay?" I inquired with concern, before recognizing the shape of a tiny kitten.

"I must seem quite melancholy," Ariadne sighed, dabbing at her eyes with the sleeve of her shirt. "I'm not sure you will care to hear about my sadness, but I must explain the situation."

I blinked with surprise, for I had not expected Ariadne to defend her emotions. I assumed she would ask me to leave the garden at once. After all, I was never comfortable with the idea of speaking to a stranger about my sorrows. It was a wonder how anyone could deal with such a thing.

"I don't want you to think I simply enjoy wallowing in self-pity." Ariadne shrugged as she wiped away another tear and glanced down at the kitten. "Penelope belongs to my friend, Juniper. She is arriving late to the Academy this year, and she has given me the task of caring for the kitten while she is gone. I did not want to leave the creature alone in my household—my younger siblings would torture the poor thing. The Academy staff checks the dormitories for this type of thing, so I have been keeping Penelope in the garden until the students are settled."

Ariadne's gray eyes watched me carefully, as though she feared I might reveal her secret. My roommate was keeping this animal without the permission of the headmistress. Although I did not care for such an idea, the girl was acting with good intentions. She deserved a trustworthy friend.

"You have to promise you will not tell anyone about this. I cannot risk the trouble that it would bring me," Ariadne said. "My parents already pay enough for me to attend this school, and they expect me to follow the rules."

It was clear that Ariadne was missing her best friend. Otherwise, her headstrong attitude would have never permitted such a conversation. She was suffering through one of the greatest trials in life, which I had grown to recognize as loneliness. My heart ached for the teenage girl, and I decided to make an effort to be her new friend.

"I promise I won't tell anyone about this cat, as long as you will sit with me at lunch for the rest of the semester."

Ariadne's eyes crinkled into a smile as she laughed. The cold wind was interrupted by a warm summer breeze, which hushed the whispers of the coming autumn.

CHAPTER NINE

I t was nearing dusk as the evening breeze blew softly
against my skin. I buttoned up my thin sweater. My
feet had been carrying me toward the castle steps,
when I passed one of the locked stone towers. My eyes
caught sight of a narrow path that led away from the
castle and into the forest. I stopped in my tracks and
took a quick glance around before heading down the
gentle slope. After peering down the path, I could have
sworn I heard a soft rustle in the bushes.

The woods were dark and foreboding in comparison
to the spectacular castle that stood in my presence. I
did not remember the forest looking so grotesque. The
tall and beautiful oaks seemed suddenly twisted, as
though countless terrifying creatures dwelled beneath
the canopy.

The woodlands were almost entirely dark, despite the shining trace of sunset that hung low in the distance. Curiosity drew me in. As I embraced the scenery with open eyes, my steps gradually led me down the forest path. I had never believed the woods were a place to fear, until I heard the low and distinctive howl. Darkness suddenly began to overwhelm me.

A bright flame ignited in my hand as I tilted my head upward. The night stars were nearly invisible through the treetops. Even the silver moonlight did not dare show its face in the haunted woods. My eyes trailed across the branches from below the shadowed canopy. It seemed as though my flames were the only source of light. I heard the rustling once more, but it was closer this time. My gaze scanned the forest that surrounded me.

I suddenly noticed a large pair of golden eyes, which had appeared out of the darkness. My heart skipped a beat. Dirt crunched beneath my boots as I backed down the forest path. Even so, the creature was moving forward much faster than I was running backward. I heard a voice growl and held my hand up to see if I could get a better look at what might be the cause of my death. A doglike muzzle appeared just beneath a pair of glowing eyes as the animal bolted toward me. Every muscle in my body had braced for an attack; however, a few moments passed without the sharp pain of teeth ripping through my flesh.

I opened my eyes to see the beast standing before me. His breath smelled of peppermint, rather than the rotting meat on his teeth. The creature's eyes reminded me of the wolf-girl from my class with Professor Barrington. I suspected the animal was one of the Guardians of Aisling. The creature was not a wolf, but he was a tall and burly wolfhound. I heard a deep rumble and almost expected the animal to bark; however, he began to speak in a rough sort of voice.

"What are you doing out here in the night?" he questioned, eyeing the flame that burned in my right hand. "You must be a student of the Academy for Gifted Youth."

"Y—yes," I stuttered as the large dog stared.

"What are you thinking? A young girl should not be wandering the Night Oak Forest this late in the evening," he barked, as if it should have been obvious.

I remained silent. I had no idea where I was standing. Despite his slightly irritating remarks, it was evident that this sharp canine knew much more about the forest than I did.

"My name is Emerson."

"I'm Alice," I replied slowly.

"Well, Alice, you may be new around here, but I must tell you this forest is not the type you'll want to be wandering through when the night sky lies overhead," Emerson spoke in the rather gruff voice that one might imagine for a dog. "These woods are home to the type of beasts you do not want to encounter while you are walking alone."

Despite the giant oak trees that grew close to the forest trail, I was beginning to feel quite exposed. After a moment of searching through my racing thoughts, I responded with an understanding nod.

"Shall I accompany you to the tree line?" Emerson snorted as he scanned the shadows.

I nodded once more. Our surroundings were beginning to grow unrecognizable in the night, and I was no longer sure of the direction that led toward the ancient castle.

"Are you one of the Guardians of Aisling?" I asked as the canine guided me through the forest.

"Indeed," Emerson huffed. "You are lucky enough to find me tonight. I was on my way back from the White Birch Forest, but I'm not due to be on patrol until tomorrow morning."

"If you don't mind my asking, why does the territory need patrols?" I questioned the hound. "Sir Barrington gave us a brief introduction to the Guardians of Aisling; however, he never discussed it in much detail."

Emerson watched me with a piercing glare. We had stopped on the edge of the forest path. Something told me the canine questioned his ability to trust me. He wasn't foolish. After all, I was nothing more than a young girl in a foreign land.

"Sir Barrington was wise to not tell his students about the curse," the wolfhound huffed. "Without the approval of Zara Hawthorne, I'm not authorized to speak about such a matter to any students. I suggest you find this information from within the Academy."

I looked up at the castle windows, which glowed brightly from the tree line. Each twinkling light reminded me of lanterns in the darkness. After a long moment, I noticed the large dog had vanished. The lack of company sent a spark of fear through my heart, and the emotion swiftly carried my body in the direction of the castle.

As I walked into the entrance hall, the passing time seemed to shift back into place. The castle was silent, and not a footstep could be heard. After tiptoeing across the smooth marble flooring, I halted in front of the dining hall doors. My amber eyes peered through the tiny glass window. Dinner had started nearly ten minutes ago. Although it was only my first day at the Academy, it seemed like I had already formed a reputation for late arrivals.

Zara's distant voice echoed as she stood behind the podium on the other side of the dining hall. Without a moment of hesitation, I opened the door and stepped into the room. The headmistress paused as everyone turned to stare in my direction. My face burned as my cheeks began to flush. I smiled with embarrassment before hurrying over to the empty chair beside my twin sister. After a moment, Zara cleared her throat, and all eyes turned back to her. My sister continued to watch me with an expression of confusion.

"Where have you been?" Emery whispered. "Kade and I studied in Lancaster Hall, but you weren't there."

"I was exploring," I replied.

"Alone?" Emery questioned.

I nodded in response.

Violet, Kade, and Ronan sat across from us, watching our interaction with dull eyes. As we began to eat

71

our dinner, the hall gradually flooded with the conversations of the Academy students. My sister placed her delicate hand over a steaming bowl of soup. After a brief moment, her dinner had cooled to just the right temperature. She took a careful sip from the spoon.

"Where did you explore?" Kade asked me as she removed her green jacket, revealing a pair of black wings.

"I walked over to the courtyard for a bit," I responded, before drinking a sip of peppermint tea. "Do you have any idea what the locked towers contain?"

"The four stone towers?" Violet asked with a sudden spark of interest.

I nodded in response.

"Many myths have been told about the towers," Kade began. "They were built nearly a century ago, and nobody has been able to open the doors since the first headmaster. Each tower is rumored to hide a terrible beast, although I don't believe such things."

"The towers are an ancient mystery, which very few of the professors dare to speak about," added Ronan. "I suppose they don't want any of the students to tamper with the doors."

"My father once told me the tower chooses the person who enters," said Violet.

Upon walking through the door of Lancaster Hall, Augusta greeted us from the seat that rested behind her

72

typewriter. The lounge was silent, and few girls studied in the silent corners.

"Good evening, girls," Augusta said, lifting her eyes to examine the three of us. Her curly brown hair had been tied in separate buns on each side of her head. They stuck out like sprouts beside her ears, but nobody in the room looked at her with more than a second glance.

As we hurried into our chamber, each of us dropped our bags near the door. After grabbing a book from the top of my trunk, I attempted to find peace between the pages of a story. Nevertheless, my curiosity was wide awake.

"Do either of you know anything about the forest that borders the school grounds?" I asked my friends.

"That depends on which one you are talking about," Kade responded. "The White Birch Forest or the Night Oak Forest?"

"I'm not sure," I responded thoughtfully. "It was very dark and gloomy. It seemed as if all the light had been stripped from the forest floor."

Emery sat cross-legged on her bed, listening carefully to our conversation. I wished she had been with me, for I missed our wonderful adventures together. We had been so busy since school began.

"I'm sure you are referring to the Night Oak Forest," Kade informed me. "The White Birch Forest is nothing of that sort." Her blue eyes seemed to darken a bit, and her voice dropped into a deep tone. It was clear that she did not want to be overheard.

"The Night Oak Forest is both utterly terrifying and extraordinarily beautiful, although this all depends on the time when you are traveling through," Kade explained. "During the daylight hours, the Night Oak Forest is home to abundant streams, beautiful birds, and towering oak trees. But the forest is dark and fearsome in the night. It is home to some of the most fearsome creatures in all of Aisling. These beasts have recently been straying from the woodland border. This is the reason the Guardians of Aisling have been scheduled for intensive patrol."

"What happens to the monsters when the sun begins to rise?" Emery asked, displaying an expression I had not seen for many years. "Do they hide?"

"They vanish," Kade spoke briskly, "like nightmares themselves."

CHAPTER TEN

The month of October arrived in a dusty haze of gold. The trees began to glisten as the crisp autumn air left the forest in a radiant blanket of leaves. It was not the end of summer warmth and sunshine, but it was the beginning of cozy socks and dappled afternoons.

My sixteenth birthday would be arriving soon, and the vial around my neck could finally be opened. I had received word that Lancaster Hall was planning a surprise party, for a few of the female students were terrible at keeping secrets. The dormitory had discovered the fact that my twin sister and I shared our birthday with Ariadne Moss.

I began to grow acquainted with the endless maze of hallways that the old castle contained. The other students were always friendly, and the professors seemed to lighten as the year continued.

Each of our teachers were very different individuals. For example, Oliver O'Reilly was a funny and carefree teacher, and he acted more like a student than a professor. He lived by the most popular Academy policy, which states that students were required to call their teachers by no more than their first name. Many of the new students did not understand this concept; however, Oliver was sure to ignore them until they caught on.

Furthermore, I had grown to know professors such as Sir Theodore Barrington. The white-haired man possessed a grumpy and cavalier face, which closely resembled that of an elderly forest elf. Sir Barrington was quite the opposite of Oliver, and he insisted that each of us call him by his formal name.

❦❦❦

It was a cold October evening when I greeted my friends at the edge of the Night Oak Forest. The trees were mellow and full of life, although I was unable to forget the night when I first stepped onto the forest path.

"What are we doing here?"

"This is how you get to the village," Violet responded as the dirt began to crunch beneath our boots.

The forest appeared to be incredibly different than before. The canopy no longer sheltered the glowing eyes of insidious creatures, as it now held the nests of peculiar songbirds. The evening sun shone brightly through the treetops, and dappled upon the forest floor. A tiny stream ran between the tree roots. Occasionally, we needed to cross a small wooden bridge, as the water had grown too wide to jump across.

After a long trek through the forest, we came to a halt at the edge of the tree line. My eyes widened with amazement. The Night Oak Forest bordered a gentle valley, which was home to an extraordinary village.

"Welcome to the village of Willowcrest," Violet spoke with a smile.

CHAPTER ELEVEN

illowcrest Village was a magnificent place. Each of the shops had been painted a variety of bright colors. The cobblestone road held a peculiar sparkle from the reflections of stained glass. Each window displayed enchanted trinkets, gemstones, and some of the strangest flowers I had encountered. Gifted people of all ages roamed the streets, and the air bustled with conversation.

"The Moss Shop is our first destination," announced Violet, pointing toward a tiny store on the other side of the road. Its thatched roof was covered in an abundance of moss, which reminded me of the fairy houses from my childhood.

Dodging wagons, horses, and fellow pedestrians, we made our way across the street. The village was beautiful; however, it was quite different from the rest of Aisling. The quiet countryside seemed oceans away from the crowded road.

As we made our way up the steps of the old mossy store, a flickering candlelight danced in the window. Violet reached for the door, although it quickly swung back in our direction. A few of us grabbed her arms to keep her from falling off the porch.

"I'm so sorry!" Ariadne stood in the doorway with a large box in her hands. "Are you hurt?"

Violet was rubbing her knee, although she straightened up and managed to fake a smile. Her eyes had transformed into a deep shade of lilac, which resembled her tangled hair. Constellations of tiny blue dots were beginning to scatter across her irises. I knew she was in more pain than she cared to admit.

"Are you sure?" Ariadne glanced at the rest of us as she walked down the steps.

"I'm all right, Ariadne. Don't worry about it." Violet nodded as she pulled open the door, and the rest of us followed her inside.

"I barely ever see that girl outside of class," said Emery, shutting the door behind us.

"Ariadne spends most of her extra time working here," Ronan responded. "Her family owns the store."

At first glance, the Moss Shop appeared to be very small. Nevertheless, it was remarkably crowded. At the front of the store was a giant oak desk, where a long line of people trailed away from the cashier. The walls were lined with bookshelves, fabric, and other materials.

As Ronan wandered through the aisles, each item he passed began to float toward the ceiling. His sister followed him, grabbing random objects from the air and placing them back on the shelves. The teenage boy was completely oblivious.

"Luckily, his sister has wings."

Violet had suddenly appeared beside me. As she watched with a hint of amusement, her eyes shifted into a bright shade of blue. I nodded slowly before drifting toward the other end of the store. The purple-haired girl followed with careful strides.

"I can't find any petalstone," Emery said as she rushed toward us. "It isn't on any of the shelves. Do you suppose they ran out?"

Violet shook her head and wandered over to the counter. People of all ages waited to make their payment to the old shopkeeper. Blue coins jingled in the pockets of every cloak. Despite the many expressions of dismay, my friend hurried to the front of the unbroken line.

"Good morning, Mr. Moss," Violet greeted the man behind the counter. "I'm very sorry to interrupt, but do you happen to know where I might find a few boxes of petalstone?"

The man's stern gaze seemed to lighten after Violet's apology. He led us to a small door in the back of the room. After a moment of searching his coat pocket, the shopkeeper retrieved an old iron key. He placed it in the keyhole and swung open the door.

"Impossible," I whispered.

The door had led us to a large hall. Glass display cases were spread out in rows before us, each containing a precious stone or trinket. Great spiral staircases led to a second floor, which held a capacious library. I hoped the pages would answer all my questions, as the hall was twice the size of the building I had entered.

Emery's gaze sparkled as her cheeks crinkled into a smile. As she ran off to continue her search, my imagination wandered over to the library. Any new book from this realm had the gift of captivating my mind. The binding was simply too difficult to close.

I wandered between the bookshelves until I began to feel like a lost girl. The library appeared to be deserted, but I eventually came across a familiar young woman. I glanced at her once more, pretending to hide my nose behind a book. The woman's identity did not resonate with me until her sapphire eyes greeted mine.

"Hello, Alice!" Zara spoke.

I greeted her with a smile.

"I've wanted to formally introduce myself to you and your sister," said Zara, placing another book in her basket.

I remained silent.

"You both have fascinating Gifts," the headmistress continued. "Twins aren't usually Gifted with such connected powers."

I was not sure what the headmistress was trying to tell me. I did not see much of a connection between the Gifts of my sister and me, for the elements of fire and water always mimicked our opposite personalities. It was common knowledge that no one had ever received the same Gift. Zara seemed to be searching my eyes for the answer to an unasked question. I was preparing to respond, but someone called my name.

"It sounds like your presence is needed elsewhere." Zara smiled as she adjusted the heavy basket in her arms. "I will be sure to meet with the two of you soon."

I nodded in return before placing my book back on the shelf. Something about that short conversation stuck with me. I tried to push it away, but I knew Zara had seen something different in my sister and me. In a realm of people who were known for their differences, the headmistress had noticed something rare. I was not sure if this was something desirable.

CHAPTER TWELVE

Several days had passed, although I was unable to rid my mind of the words that Zara had spoken in the library. I sought to dismiss our conversation as normal; however, I could not convince myself of such a thing. The headmistress's words seemed to hide a message.

The study of Gifts began to take up my afternoon hours, and caused me to be more interested during class time. I felt as if I was neglecting my sister a bit. Nevertheless, she did not seem to notice, as her time was now devoted to our realm exploration class, and our bedroom had transformed into a museum of ancient maps.

I already knew every person was born with an individual Gift. However, for many years, the magical realm has separated each gift into a particular class or category. There are fewer than one hundred different types of Gifts, which are divided into the Common, Oddities, and Rare Gifts.

For example, Kade has the Gift of Wings, which means that she is classified in the Flight Category. This group is considered an Oddity because the types of wings that exist happen to vary. Some Gifted individuals have been born with fairy or insect wings, while Kade was born with feathered wings. This creates more room for other people, and it means that my friend is not the only person with the Gift of Flight.

Emery was Gifted with the ability to manipulate the element of water, while I was Gifted with the element of fire. Although we are twins, we are no exception to the rule of individual Gifts. We are placed under the same Elemental Category, which represents only four powers. Elementals are considered one of the rarest in the history of magic. The last Elemental existed more than three-hundred years before we were born.

❧❦❧❦

The forest colors flashed past me in a blur, and streaks of sunlight peaked through the trees. The morning breeze blew gently through my hair as my delicate hand dangled out the window. Everything seemed normal until I noticed the absence of freckles on my skin.

The carriage began to bounce as we pulled to a slow halt. I was alone with a light stack of suitcases, which sat on the floor beneath me. As I called out in a voice that was not my own, I was answered by the gruff response of the coachman at the head of the carriage. His inaudible sentence was quickly cut short.

Something was terribly wrong.

A certain silence hung in the air, which sent shivers up the sides of my arms. Without quite receiving permission, my hand reached for the carriage door. I stepped out into the forest on slightly taller legs. As I peeked around the big horses, the world faded into darkness around me.

I woke with a scream, finding my sister's pale hand held gently against my forehead. Tears were streaming down my face as my body became arrested in a series of convulsing gasps. Nightmares were never something I frequently encountered, although they were always hauntingly realistic.

"Are you all right, Alice?"

I looked up to see the concern in Emery's expression. After glancing at the clock, I realized we were nearly late for our first class of the day. I struggled to gain control of my racing heartbeat.

"I'm fine," I responded before pulling myself out of bed. "It was just a nightmare."

"You've always had some of the worst." Emery nodded sympathetically.

After quickly throwing on a dress and one of my favorite wool sweaters, I grabbed my book bag and followed Emery out of the dormitories. As we walked down the old castle passageway, gazes seemed to catch on me like thorns upon a Sunday dress. Some of them felt less comfortable than others.

The rest of the morning seemed to drag as though my body were recovering from a night of insomnia. My Gift was becoming hard to control, as my mind drifted through a layer of fog. The nightmare returned in haunting flashbacks, which felt almost as real as the dream itself.

"Are you okay, Alice?"

I looked up to see Ronan standing before me with a spark of concern in his gaze. My mind was racing in a million directions, like a field of comets across the night sky. I realized that my body had come to a halt in the middle of the crowded corridor. Ronan's eyes were dusted with concern as I dared to meet his gaze. He gestured to the flames that danced upon my hands.

"I haven't been able to stop," I told him with a simple shrug. "It has been going on all morning."

"Where is your sister?"

"I haven't seen her since we left the dormitory," I responded as my friend watched me with a thoughtful expression.

My hands were shaking, and my fiery Gift was out of control. The chaos terrified me. Perhaps the nightmare had triggered a memory from the past.

"Follow me," Ronan said before grabbing my hand and leading me through the crowd of students.

CHAPTER THIRTEEN

We hurried down the castle halls and through several hidden doorways. Unreadable faces rushed past me in a haze of dull colors. I did not have any clue where the headmistress's office resided, but I knew my friend was taking me there.

Ronan held my hand tightly as we ran up an ever-lasting spiral stairwell. We eventually came to a dark and unlit hallway. Near the end of the passage stood a sparkling silver door, which illuminated a path through the darkness.

"It's probably best for you to go in alone," Ronan whispered.

I nodded and made my way down the hall. Stopping in front of the door, I held my hand up with hesitation. The entrance began to creak open before my knuckle had the chance to touch the surface of the wood.

The headmistress's office was unlike anything I had ever seen. I did not feel that such a place should be called an office, for the word was bland and held no justice. The room contained dozens of towering bookshelves, which had been built entirely out of wood from the depths of the White Birch Forest. White marble beams soared toward the arched ceiling, and glass windows sparkled and shimmered in the afternoon light.

After a long moment, I felt something brush against my leg. I glanced down to see a white rabbit sniffing gently at my boots. He looked up at me with wide eyes and floppy ears. I stroked the tiny creature atop his head. Something about the rabbit seemed to remind me of home.

"I see you have met my friend."

I jumped as a voice spoke from behind me. As I glanced over my shoulder, I noticed Zara was seated behind an enormous desk in the back of the room. I looked around awkwardly before taking a seat in front of her.

"He is quite an extraordinary creature," she continued. "You won't find very many rabbits like him in Aisling. When I was a little girl, I found him wandering the edge of the White Birch Forest. I assume he came here from your world."

We watched in silence as the tiny rabbit wandered the room before plopping down to take a nap. I looked back at Zara to see her smile with admiration for the little creature.

"How can I help you, Alice?" Zara asked, noticing my obvious agitation. Her sapphire eyes glanced down at the glimmering flames in both of my hands.

"I've had quite a peculiar nightmare," I told her. "It felt incredibly real and has been haunting my mind."

Words poured out of my mouth, like Earl Grey from a porcelain teapot. I hoped the headmistress would be able to understand. When I finally finished explaining, I was hesitant to meet the woman's gaze. As she uttered a laugh, I looked up to see a smile spread wide across her pale face.

"I had the same trouble when I was your age," the headmistress told me.

"You did?" I responded with surprise written across my freckled cheeks.

"I certainly did," Zara said with an expression of nostalgia. "I used to have terrible nightmares. They did not come often, but they were always quite intimidating."

Zara looked me in the eyes for a long moment. Her sapphire gaze held an expression that I was unable to read. It seemed as if she wanted me to say something more; however, there was little room for sanity in further words.

"My Gift has become unmanageable," I explained as my ginger hair began to spark. "I don't know what to do, and I feel like there is something wrong with me."

"Nightmares have the dreadful effect of captivating our minds during the waking hours," Zara told me. "Nevertheless, they are merely fiction."

I settled into a state of silence. The headmistress had spoken the truth I needed to hear from another person. The flashbacks gradually began to fade as my Gift fell back into place, although the haunting memories still held their place within me.

CHAPTER FOURTEEN

When I finally left the office, Ronan was nowhere to be found. After wandering through the maze of castle corridors, I managed to find my way back to the entrance hall. The air hung silent, and the stairwell stood abandoned. As I made my way down the hardwood steps, the glittering sunlight danced through the windows. The evening sun was setting, and the castle would soon be illuminated by the light of a thousand lanterns.

As I hurried over to the dining hall, the door attendants greeted me and swung the heavy doors wide. I scanned the tables for my group of friends, but it was nearly impossible to find them in the crowded hall. My gaze eventually caught on the lavender hair of Violet Holloway, who was huddled at the end of a table.

After taking a seat between Ronan and Violet, I began to notice their abnormal behavior. The O'Reilly twins were quite reserved, and Violet poked at her food in silence. Our table seemed to be the center of attention, as the other students continued to throw glances in our direction.

"Is everything all right?" I inquired.

For a brief moment, I was not sure anyone was going to respond. Apprehension appeared in the back of my mind, while Kade raised her eyes to look at me. "Something horrible has happened," she whispered. The whites of her eyes were a faint shade of pink, and her cheeks were damp with tears.

Every person seemed to be focused on Violet, who poked at her dinner with an unreadable expression. Her eyes reminded me of an iridescent fabric that changed color from different angles. It seemed as though the material had been flung from an unbearable height, as her eyes changed color with every gust of wind.

"Juniper is gone. She's gone!" Violet exclaimed before quickly dropping her fork and storming out of the dining hall.

"Who is Juniper?" I asked the rest of my friends, as every student turned to stare at us.

"She is Violet's cousin," Ronan explained. "Juniper was supposed to be entering the Academy late this semester, due to a visit to one of the isles off the coast. Late this afternoon, Violet was informed that Juniper's carriage was attacked while she was passing through the Night Oak Forest."

Ariadne had told me about this new girl. The tiny kitten in our room belonged to the missing student. Violet was missing her cousin, and Ariadne was missing her best friend. My mind began to run over the number of ways this accident might have occurred.

"When the scene was discovered, the girl was nowhere to be found," Kade added.

Violet's footsteps echoed up the stairwell in the entrance hall, breaking through the silence of the dining room. The door was still swinging in and out of the archway, while her fork lay thrown across the plate. My mind was beginning to pile high with questions.

"Does anyone know what attacked her?" I asked.

"We were told it was a creature of the night," Emery suddenly spoke up. A haunted expression was hidden behind her sparkling blue eyes. It reminded me of the look across my face on the day when we had been told to come here.

"If Juniper was attacked during the day, how could it have been a creature of the night?" I inquired, tapping my freckled fingers on the smooth table.

"That is precisely what everyone else has been wondering," said Kade. "It seems impossible, but the evidence has been found."

"We have been told to keep out of the Night Oak Forest until we are notified it is safe to pass through," Ronan added as he took the last bite from his plate.

93

I do not think any of us managed to sleep through the night. Our thoughts were too worried about the unknown fate of Juniper Stone. I may not have known Violet's cousin, but that did not reduce my concern for a missing Gifted. The girl had disappeared without a trace. I knew the darkness of the Night Oak Forest, although I could not imagine what it would be like to be lost in its depths.

As the next few days passed, not a trace of Juniper Stone was discovered. The search patrols had scoured every corner of the Night Oak Forest, but the girl was never found. Many people began to lose hope after a while. However, despite the pain in her misty eyes, Ariadne still managed to smile.

It was a Tuesday morning when Emery and I were wandering through the castle halls. Students of all ages pushed through the doorways, on the way to their next class. Violet's face swooped past us in the crowded corridor. Although we exchanged eye contact, her face remained as blank as a fresh sheet of paper.

Emery turned to watch our friend with sympathy. Despite her lilac hair and kaleidoscopic gaze, Violet could not help but look miserable. I turned around and followed her down the hall. The passageway was crowded, and we were the only people heading the opposite direction. Thus, I grew used to the constant shoving that occurred. I heard someone call my name and glanced over my shoulder to see Emery hurrying after me.

"Alice! Where are you going? We will be late for class," my sister spoke in her usual gentle voice, but this time it had a slight edge.

"We cannot leave her like this, Emery. It isn't fair to anyone." I gestured to Violet, who was about to round the corner beside the large stairwell.

Emery looked at me for a moment before we began to run after our friend. We had to do something. We had to find Juniper. This had gone on for far too long. As we came to the top of the stairwell, we noticed Violet had already reached the floor of the entrance hall. We hurried down the stairs, taking the last four steps in a leap.

Sage Pine was sitting at the bottom of the staircase, accompanied by a dark-haired boy our age. They watched us behind suspicious golden eyes.

"Please stop, Violet!" Emery shouted as we followed her through the giant castle doors.

I was not sure if she heard our voices, but Violet kept walking until she reached the end of the steps. She looked even more sorrowful up close. Her eyes had settled into an expressionless and dull shade of gray. It seemed as though her soul were locked in a windowless room, illuminated only by the ray of light that shone through a crack beneath the door.

"What are you doing here?" Violet inquired wistfully. "Shouldn't you be in class?"

"I suppose we could ask you the same question," Emery replied.

"I know Juniper is out there." Violet sighed as her eyes flashed like the colors of the setting sun. "The Guardians told me that if they don't find her within the next few days, they will be calling off the forest search. I don't know how people can give up with such ease."

I gazed upon the vast expanse of fields and forests, which stood before the mossy castle. If the missing girl was out there, she could be anywhere between the quilted meadows and White Birch Forest. The search patrol was only scanning the place where she had disappeared.

"Why didn't I think of this before?" I exclaimed as my ginger hair blew gently across my face.

"What are you talking about?"

Violet and Emery watched me with flickering blue eyes. I knew their hearts still held a piece of hope. We could not allow ourselves to give up on faith.

"Meet us in the courtyard at midnight," I told Violet with a smile.

"Tomorrow is your birthday, Alice!" she called after me, as if the occasion should change my mind. I waved a hand in dismissal before hurrying back through the castle doors. We were going to find Juniper Stone. It did not matter if the search patrol had stopped looking, for I had developed a remarkable plan.

CHAPTER FIFTEEN

Soon after we arrived in Lancaster Hall, Augusta stormed into our room. Her usual cheerful expression was masked by a look of anger and frustration. The surface of her freckled cheeks was dusted with a bright shade of pink.

"You must report to Professor Hawthorne's office," Augusta demanded.

I looked up from my textbook and glanced over to Emery, who was shuffling through the trunk at the end of her bed. I assumed this was punishment for skipping class to comfort Violet, who was likely on her way to the office as well. We hurried past Augusta and through the open doorway. Emery looked quite nervous as she picked at her nails, avoiding eye contact with any of the other girls.

"Don't assume you are so easily out of the picture, Ariadne Moss." Augusta raised her voice.

Ariadne lifted one eyebrow and dropped a large stack of books on the floor. Our roommate had not skipped class with us. As we made our way through Lancaster Hall, I began to wonder why we had been summoned.

We hurried through the corridors and past the towering, wood stairwell. Everyone seemed to be drowning in a haze of thoughts. It felt as though my vision were clouded by the questions that raced through my mind. My sister's eyes held a grave look of concern, although Ariadne's expression was indecipherable.

We eventually arrived in the hidden corridor that led to the headmistress's office. Darkness engulfed the air, and the only light was the glimmer beneath the door at the end of the hallway. I flicked my wrist to create a flame before leading my friends down the hall. The sparkling door that had once illuminated the hidden entrance was now as black as night. Something in my gut told me this meeting was not just about skipping our class.

After taking a deep breath, I grabbed hold of the gemstone handle and pushed the door open. Despite my nervous mind, the act of entering Zara's office seemed just as extraordinary as the very first time. I glanced over at the large desk. The headmistress was not seated in her chair, although the old table was stacked high with piles of dusty books.

"Good afternoon," I heard a voice speak out from over my shoulder. We turned to see Zara standing neatly in the center of the room.

"I would like to thank you for agreeing to meet with me this evening. I've gathered us together to speak about a growing concern," Zara spoke in her always-proper accent, but her voice now held an irreplaceable edge. "This situation has not been publicized to any of the other Academy students; therefore, I must ask that you keep it a secret."

"I get the feeling this isn't about skipping class," Emery commented after a moment of silence.

"I'm sure there will be another opportunity for you to deal out those excuses, but we will pretend it never happened." Zara laughed.

"As I'm sure each of you already know, one of the Academy students has gone missing. Her cousin, Violet Holloway, has probably informed you that the carriage was attacked as Juniper made her way through the Night Oak Forest. This incident occurred during the daylight hours."

We each nodded in response.

"This is a great concern, as each of the deadly beasts who roam the forest at night have been known to disappear at the break of dawn. They are prohibited from returning until the sunlight disappears," explained Zara.

Something about the conversation was making my anxiety rise. Although she was not aware of her actions, the headmistress was hiding behind hesitation. Why did she bring us to the office?

"For many centuries, the realm of Aisling has been slowly deteriorating. It began with the magical creatures; many of our majestic, kind, and enchanted beasts have started to disappear. It wasn't until about a century ago when the monsters began to roam the night." Professor Hawthorne's voice pierced through the deafening silence. "We have not seen the curse progress very much until now. Not all of the dark creatures are disappearing during the daytime; therefore, it is becoming unsafe to wander through the Night Oak Forest."

No one spoke for a very long moment. A million questions were racing through my mind. As I glanced over at my twin sister, she stared expressionlessly at the lacing of her leather boots. Zara watched us, patiently waiting for a response.

"How did this start?" Ariadne finally asked.

"A long time ago, before the Academy existed, there was a man known as Professor Silas Casper. He committed his entire life to the study of Gifted people. His goal was to make a creative and understandable way of learning for the Gifted children. After some time, Silas met an extraordinary mentor who taught him the secrets of the realm. They set out to create a school for the children of the Gifted society." Zara's eyes glistened as she gazed out the castle window. "They chose this brilliant castle over every other location in the realm of Aisling. It was truly a dream; however, a problem soon arose.

"Wolfgang Gregory was a man with unpopular views of the Gifted society," the headmistress continued. "He felt that the realm of Aisling lacked the element of social ranking. He believed people of common categorized Gifts were superior to the individuals with rare Gifts, and this is how Gift classification was brought into existence. In the land where everyone was equal, Wolfgang sought to promote the idea that one person was better than the next, simply because they possessed a different talent."

"Aisling has never had a ruler?" Emery inquired.

I suppose the idea did seem a bit foreign to us. In our world, every territory was ruled under a government. Another human was always in charge of the countries, states, and societies. It was strange to think the Gifted people had lived otherwise.

"We have never found it necessary, for the people of Aisling are generally quite peaceful." Zara laughed. "If an issue arises, the situation is always handled by the Order of Birch at Castle Moss."

Professor Blakely Biddle often spoke about the Order of Birch in our Realm History class. With ancient stone walls towering above the middle of the White Birch Forest, Castle Moss was the center of Aisling's government. Whenever there was a decision to be made, that was where it took place.

"Wolfgang Gregory realized the Academy was against everything he believed, and he wanted nothing more than to witness its destruction. Silas was aware of the concern the establishment had brought to his enemies; however, he did not expect to witness action," Zara continued. "Unfortunately, our founder was

101

wrong. Wolfgang managed to capture a rare bog troll, which he tortured into setting a terrible curse on this land."

"What does this have to do with us?" Ariadne spoke in a quiet voice.

The headmistress shifted in her seat. Her sapphire gaze wandered into the distance, as though she were watching something that was invisible to the naked eye.

"The prophecy has brought you here," Zara sighed after a moment.

My gaze shifted toward my sister. Her misty blue eyes looked back at me in confusion.

"What prophecy?" Ariadne questioned, as if she were able to read all three of our minds.

I noticed movement out of the corner of my eye, and glanced up to see a book floating across the room. It came from the direction of the sun-dappled bookshelves that stood in the back of the room. I was convinced I was beginning to see things, although Zara eventually raised her gaze. The dusty book dropped from midair, landing perfectly in the headmistress's hands before she placed it on the ancient desk. Zara opened the page at random, looking up at the three of us with an unreadable expression. I watched as she waved her hand in a circular motion, and the pages began to turn with graceful control. There was no need to glance at my sister, as her eyes would always be wide with amazement.

"Almost sixteen years ago, a new page appeared in this book. It did not have a number or belong to a particular chapter in the story—it simply appeared,"

Zara explained as she traced her slender finger down the page. "It tells us about a prophecy that involves four elementally Gifted students, who are destined to return Aisling to peace."

The air was settled in a peculiar state of silence. My eyes flickered curiously between the faces of my fellow students. I was sure my racing heartbeat was the only movement in the room. The suspense was tormenting my imaginative mind, which was quick to assume the result of our fate.

"The three of you are part of this prophecy. We've known it since you were children," said Professor Hawthorne.

"Is this a joke?" Ariadne stuttered. "I've been going to this school since I was eight years old. You're telling me this *now*?"

"It was necessary to keep the prophecy a secret until we discovered the other girls," explained Zara. "Nevertheless, it seems as if we are running out of time. You must find the last elemental and complete the prophecy."

"How are we supposed to do that?" questioned Emery. "We barely talk to any of the students outside of Lancaster Hall. We will not be able to identify the last elemental among all of the students in the Academy for Gifted Youth."

"What are you talking about?" I demanded. "You can't just expect us to finish a prophecy that we hardly know anything about."

With a quick wave of her hand, Zara sent the dusty book flying back to the library maze. She turned to look at us with piercing blue eyes. "I have told you all that I know. A prophecy does not come with instructions. It is largely a matter of fate," she explained. "The fate of Aisling rests in your hands. I'm sorry I can't do more to help you find your way."

CHAPTER SIXTEEN

All my life, I knew I was different. I had always been recognized as strange and peculiar, but Aisling became the place where I felt at home. It was the only place where people accepted my unusual Gift and endless quirks. I was beginning to enjoy the feeling of fitting in with the crowd of students; however, the prophecy was pulling me away from this identity.

Although I had only arrived a few months ago, it already seemed like I carried more responsibility than the headmistress. My mind was racing. If we did not find the fourth student, the realm of Aisling was destined to crumble. I felt like I had just read a breathtaking and fantastic novel, yet I was the individual who had been living in it.

The other girls refused to speak on the journey back to Lancaster Hall; I suppose everyone was absorbing the shock. As we walked in silence, I was reminded about my plan to search for Violet's lost cousin in the most dangerous part of the realm. My sister was hesitant to follow in my footsteps, although she eventually agreed to the idea. We were running the risk of expulsion, but I believed it was the only chance Juniper had left.

As we rested in our room, I listed through the names of my fellow classmates. Not one of the children or teenagers had been Gifted with an elemental power.

All hope seemed to be lost.

Kade glanced at us from behind her thick book. She had not asked any questions since we walked through the door, although I knew she was more than curious about our interaction with the headmistress.

The afternoon light had already faded from the elaborate stained-glass windows. It was late in the night. Augusta would soon arrive to tell us that it was past our bedtime, and I did not want to be awake for such an encounter. I set the alarm for midnight and blew out the candles that illuminated my bedside table. It wasn't long before I found myself lost in the land of dreams.

I was wandering on a dimly lit path, somewhere deep within the White Birch Forest. The faint melody of a songbird traveled through the autumn breeze. Tall birches and sycamore trees rose high above me, while their branches swayed gracefully in the wind. The sound of nature was the only voice that dared to break the silence.

I was alone.

Glancing around at the wilderness that surrounded me, my amber gaze caught like a thorn on the movement in the grass. A tiny stem was beginning to rise from the ground beneath me, blooming into the shape of a delicate, pink wildflower.

I woke to the clock ringing in my ear.

Juniper.

The message of my dream had arrived with sudden force. It wasn't difficult to decipher the truth that was hidden in a few short moments. Juniper Stone was the fourth elemental! She was Gifted with nature.

I quickly turned off the alarm. As my body tumbled out of bed, the eyes of my roommates remained closed. Despite the sound of my clumsy footsteps, the other girls continued to sleep.

After throwing on my clothes and grabbing a dark cloak out of my wardrobe, I tucked my vial necklace into the collar of my shirt. It was the day of my sixteenth birthday. After three years of waiting, I could finally open the glass vial and read the mysterious note inside. Pulling the chain back out of my collar, I ran my freckled fingers down to where the cork had been tightly secured.

A sudden noise echoed from across the bedroom. I glanced up to see that Emery was waiting for me. She glanced around for a brief moment before walking toward the door. I tucked the necklace back into my collar, deciding to open it later. We hurried through the door and into the dormitory hall.

The lounge was quiet, and no one was around. It seemed like ages before we made it to the large stairwell; however, just a few strides remained before we reached the towering castle doors. I was not surprised to find them locked, and I had already planned an alternative escape path. Although many are careful to close the main doors, the caretakers are not always wise enough to lock the windows on the side of the entrance.

I slid my pale fingers beneath the glass, quietly pushing the window open. It was slightly ajar, which meant Violet was probably waiting for us. I gestured for my sister to lead the way, and with one quick jump, she landed in the garden below.

"Alice?"

I jumped at the sudden sound of a voice behind me. My sister looked up with panic in her expression. As I glanced over my shoulder, Ronan O'Reilly stood quietly on the last step of the white stairwell.

He was alone.

"Hello, Ronan," I responded with a casual smile, as though we were not attempting to sneak out a castle window. "What are you doing up already?"

"I could ask you the same question, Alice Hanley," the boy responded, allowing me to catch a glimpse of his smile through the darkness.

"I asked you first," I retorted.

"Well," Ronan responded with a brisk voice. "I was simply on my way back from the bathroom, when I heard footsteps and noticed a certain red-headed girl attempting to sneak through the front window."

It abruptly occurred to me that I had forgotten to pull the cloak over my head. If I did not tell Ronan where we were going, he was bound to inform a professor. I could not allow us to be caught, for the fate of the realm rested in our actions.

"We are on our way to meet Violet in the courtyard," I whispered, pulling the hood of my cloak over my head. "We are going to find Juniper Stone."

"Who is with you?" he questioned with a look of curiosity on his freckled face.

As I gestured out the window, the brown-haired boy glanced into the garden below.

"Hello, Ronan!" My sister greeted him with a wave as she stood beside a patch of pink rosebushes.

"We must be quiet!" I scolded her before glancing over my shoulder.

"May I come with you?" Ronan asked as I hopped through the window.

"Not unless you're up for the possibility of being expelled," I responded before stepping out of the garden.

It would seem Ronan was not worried about getting into trouble, as he followed us into the night air. The three of us ran swiftly down the cobblestone path and around the side of the castle. The night was chilly, although it bothered the others more than me. Ronan crossed his arms in an attempt to keep warm, as he was still dressed in a T-shirt and plaid pajama pants. Every shadow seemed to belong to a terrifying beast, and every rustle of the branches caused us to jump.

"Happy birthday," Ronan added as we jogged down the old stone path.

I smiled in response.

As we reached the courtyard, my hands pushed open the gate. Violet Holloway was seated on a bench in the center of the garden. My heart skipped a beat when I noticed she was not alone. As we approached, I released a sigh of relief. The unexpected figure was none other than Ariadne Moss.

"What is she doing here?" my sister asked.

"I woke up and noticed you were gone. When I walked into the lounge, I caught Violet sneaking out," Ariadne explained.

"I invited her to come," Violet told us. "Don't worry—she isn't going to tell anyone."

"How did you get here before us?" Ronan questioned.

"People often seem to forget about my unique Gift," Violet spoke as she rolled her eyes. After a moment, her gaze shifted toward me. "What is *Ronan* doing here?"

"He noticed us when we were on our way out of the castle, and he asked if he could come with us," I responded as we followed Emery through the courtyard gate.

All eyes seemed to rest on me.

"So, what is the plan?" Ronan asked as we gathered beside the stone wall.

The edge of the Night Oak Forest stood in the distance. It reminded me of an unlit room, consumed in shadows and penetrating darkness. Every once in a while, I could have sworn I noticed a creature moving, or a pair of eyes lurking in the darkness.

I turned my head to see Violet pull a thick scroll out of her bag. She unrolled it to reveal an ancient map of the realm.

"Where did you find that?" Emery gasped.

"Let's just say that sometimes it pays to forget your Realm History essay, for you are often forced to stay after class." Violet laughed.

I glanced down at the intricate map. The realm of Aisling looked quite smaller than it felt. Violet hummed as she traced her finger around the map, until it reached the location of the Academy. Her eyes flashed a sudden shade of lavender, and she began to draw a trail of stardust across the paper.

"That should be the perfect route," Violet whispered before taking her finger away from the scroll.

"This is all very well, but what happens when you try to return this artifact to Blakely Biddle?" Ronan asked as he gestured to the sparkling paper.

"If I put it there, I can certainly take it off," Violet snapped. "It's much better than getting lost at this hour."

Violet quickly rolled the scroll back up and dropped it into her bag. She was right. I did not plan what I was going to say if we were caught, and I did not need to lose a friend in the process. If we wanted to find Juniper before the sunrise, we would need to begin our journey.

After another moment of discussion, we quietly hurried down the cobblestone path. Despite the distant hoot of an owl, the midnight air was silent. I glanced over my shoulder to make sure the group was keeping up. We veered toward an old dirt trail, which led around the side of the castle. We passed the towering windows of the dining hall before making our way around one of the Four Lone Towers. Half of the group had no idea where we were going, but I was sure my plan was infallible.

CHAPTER SEVENTEEN

We walked down a steep dirt path, which had been uprooted by the trunks of towering oaks. Every step we took and every sound in the distance made my heart beat a little faster. I didn't want to be caught for sneaking out in the night, especially with the effect the curse was having on the creatures of the woods. But I could not drop the plan and go back. Whether the Gifted people knew it or not, the realm of Aisling was depending on us to find Juniper Stone.

As we came to a halt where the tall oaks greeted the bank of a clear stream, shadows lurked among the trees, hiding secrets from our eyes. I did not know what the future would bring, but I knew that life is not merely about knowledge. It is about the courage and trust we place in our stories. After everything that brought me to this moment, it was courage that kept me going.

Through the darkness came a light that illuminated the path ahead of us. My gaze wandered in search of its origin, but the radiance appeared to be coming from the forest itself. Sycamores lined the far side of the stream as each of the branches danced with the breeze. Beyond them settled a quiet meadow that was scattered with wildflowers and the early morning dew.

Emery stood silently at the edge of the stream. Her pale eyes closed as she listened to the sound of the current. As the rest of us gathered near the top of the bank, we could barely see each other through the flickering golden light. The stream was flowing fast. There was neither a bridge nor fallen tree to lead us across the water. Nevertheless, I suppose it was a fine example of the moments when Gifts come in handy.

"Is there any way you can make it easier for us to cross?" I asked my sister, as her eyes penetrated through the shadowed water.

Before Emery had the chance to respond, I noticed something move out of the corner of my eye. I turned to see a flash of purple disappear no quicker than I had caught sight of it. I glanced around at the others with a puzzled expression, before we noticed another flash of light on the far side of the stream.

Violet stood on the opposite side of the water, waving gleefully from the line of sycamore trees. Laughter escaped from my lungs. Her teleportation skills must have slipped my mind.

"I didn't know you could do that," my voice echoed across the water.

Her response came back in a puzzle I was unable to decipher. There was another sudden flash before Violet disappeared into a puff of blue smoke. Each of us looked around for a moment before the girl reappeared in the center of the group. As she stood before us, her eye color transformed into a brilliant shade of blue. She was unable to contain the laughter that filled her soul.

"Can you get us across?" I inquired.

Emery was still sitting on the bank. She had calmed the current, although I was sure none of us wanted to swim. Violet nodded in response before each of us gathered into a circle.

"I'm not going to lie. I've never done teleportation this close with more than two people." Violet sighed as we each took hands. "I'm hoping it will work."

"I think we're all hoping it will work," Ronan responded grimly.

There was a moment in between our conversation and the light that filled my gaze—a moment so quick it could have been missed. I was sure my heart had skipped a beat, for it felt like the ground below us was caving in and disappearing at the same time. The only thing that felt secure was my left hand, as it held tightly to my sister. For the first time in my life, it felt like everything was falling apart with the promise of coming back together.

Something shifted in the air. I opened my eyes to see we were now standing on the opposite side of the stream. The tall sycamores towered over us like skyscrapers in the world's largest city. As I looked across the circle, Violet's eyes faded back into a pale shade of blue.

Not wasting any time, we quickly climbed the bank and stepped into the vast meadow that stood before us. The tall grass swayed gracefully in the midnight breeze. For an ethereal moment, I could have sworn it was dancing. We had not taken more than one step into the meadow before stopping in our tracks. A high-pitched squeal echoed through my eardrums.

I felt a sudden prod at my foot and glanced down to see a tiny girl standing in the grass. Her curly blonde hair swept down upon her leaf-like dress, and she held a bouquet of wildflowers in her arms. The fairy must have been no more than four inches tall. Looking up at me with obvious annoyance, she poked my leg once more. I lifted my foot to reveal a pink flower, which was no bigger than the tiny girl. It had crumpled to the ground under the weight of my boot. As the little creature touched the stem, the delicate flower ruffled its petals and sprung back to life.

The laughter of friends faded out of focus as the tiny fairy gathered the flower in her hands. She glared at me with one last look of annoyance before disappearing into the dew-covered meadow.

"What in all of Aisling was that?" I asked.

"That was one of the droplet faeries," Violet responded as she took the lead. She was careful to watch her step as we trekked through the field.

"Many of them wander this meadow," Ariadne remarked with a hint of laughter. "They have this sort of obsession with wildflowers."

"They collect the blossoms and bring them back to their clans," Ronan added. "They use flowers to build villages on the other side of the White Birch Forest."

This was all quite fascinating; however, my mind was beginning to find itself wrapped in another situation. We had nearly made it to the White Birch Forest, but I had no idea what to do once we arrived. I was so caught up in the prophecy and search for Juniper, but I had not even considered where she might be hiding. The White Birch Forest was boundless, and there was a chance we would be searching all night. Nevertheless, as our feet dragged in the mossy soil and our eyes hung low from lack of sleep, I realized this was certainly not an option.

"I need to talk to you in private," I whispered to my sister.

After motioning for Ariadne to follow us, we wandered out of earshot from the others. I turned to face the two of them. It had occurred to me that half the people in our search party had no idea about the prophecy, and I was the only one who knew Juniper was the last elemental. My sister's blue eyes always seemed pale and indecisive to me, although they now seemed haunted by the fear of my words.

"A few moments ago, it occurred to me that I haven't been entirely honest with you," I told them. "I think there might be something you have yet to learn about the prophecy."

I had prepared myself for a dramatic reaction, but neither of my friends spoke a word. I lifted my head to see both of them watching me.

"You had the dream, didn't you?" Ariadne whispered.

My sister's eyes widened with surprise. We stared at each other with an expression of wonder. All three of us had received the dream. We each knew Juniper was the last Elemental. It bothered me, slightly, that no one else had spoken about this until now.

"We don't have any idea where she could be," Emery whispered. "We will be searching the forest all night."

"We must ask Violet," said Ariadne.

The field behind us twinkled in the darkness as all five of us stood on the forest edge. Shadows seemed to consume the activity of the meadow. The moonlight shone upon Violet as she twirled her lilac hair in thought.

"Juniper has been coming to the Academy since she was twelve years old," Violet told us quietly. "She would often disappear into the White Birch Forest, as it was the only place where she felt at home. As you can see, it is quite a distance from the school on foot. However, my cousin had a soul that could not be confined by the castle walls."

"She must be here." Ronan gestured to the vast expanse of woodland. "We just need to find her."

Violet nodded as we stepped beyond the line of birch trees. When my boot landed upon the mossy soil, reality transformed into a strange fairytale. Tall white trees surrounded us with dark eyes, which were hidden in the bark of their trunks. The forest was silent as golden leaves glistened in the moonlight. Even amongst the darkness of the night, the ancient wood was illuminated from its core. Each of us began to spread apart, for we no longer carried the fear of being alone.

We wandered through the forest for what felt like an eternity. I began to wonder when someone would notice we were gone. My eyes searched carefully around every corner, yet there was not a footprint left of Juniper Stone. As I stepped around one of the old birches, I caught a glimpse of a small brown hare before it scurried off into the bushes. This seemed peculiar to me, for the creatures of Aisling were rarely startled by the presence of humans.

"Something is wrong," I whispered.

I looked over my shoulder to see Emery sitting cross-legged in the grass. In front of her was a small group of droplet faeries, who huddled tightly together, carrying bundles of wildflowers in their strong arms. Emery watched them with an expression of fascination, although the faeries were pointing in my direction. Their inaudible conversations confirmed the worry that rested upon each of their brows. Turning my gaze toward the other end of the forest path, I noticed the movement of several bushes at the foot of one particular tree. A sudden squeal erupted from behind me, and the droplet faeries came streaming past.

"What in all of Aisling was that?" Ronan asked, darting around one of the trees.

"Willoughby, is that you?"

There was a moment of silence before Violet ran past me, accompanied by the petite figure of Ariadne. Her bright blue eyes were flashing purple as she came to a halt before the bushes.

"Who is Willoughby?" Emery questioned.

The branches began to rustle once again, before the droplet faeries came running out. Held high above their heads was a tiny yet plump creature, who closely resembled a forest troll. He was dressed in leather trousers with a moss coat around his shoulders. I watched with amusement as he flailed wildly above the strong faeries.

"Put me down, ye filthy creatures!" the troll demanded.

The droplet faeries released the creature just a few feet in front of us. He dropped heavily to the ground before dusting off his coat.

"Willoughby, it *is* you!" Violet greeted the troll with delight.

"Yes, 'tis I," the troll groaned as he raised his head to look at us. His bushy brows just barely hid two sparkling, viridescent eyes. "What other troll do ye know who is bossed around by the droplet faeries?"

"We need your help," Violet told him curtly. "You've probably heard Juniper is missing. Has there been any sign of her?"

"Perhaps," Willoughby responded smoothly. "But you know my memory is quite poor. I'm not sure I recall."

The old troll looked around in thought for a moment. The creature wanted payment for the discovery of Juniper Stone. I had to admit Willoughby was smarter than I expected. Even so, the droplet faeries were listening to his words, and their tiny bodies were beginning to surround him.

"We don't have time for your games," Ariadne spoke sternly to the old troll. "We shall only release you if you help us find our way."

"Fine," Willoughby responded curtly. "Just don't come crying to me if ye don't like what ye find."

Willoughby led us off the forest path and through another field of peculiar wildflowers. The droplet faeries followed us in haste as they clutched their flower bundles tightly to their chests. They followed with remarkable speed. In fact, it seemed like they knew exactly where Willoughby was going. It was almost as if the old troll had been a messenger for those without a voice.

We eventually came to an emerald hollow that was settled amidst the wildflowers and misty morning air. What we found there was far from what we expected.

CHAPTER EIGHTEEN

Sometimes, when someone is lost or gone for a very long time, you find yourself imagining what it will be like when you meet them again. Often scattered with frantic hugs and tears of joy, the visions are not always realistic. It was evident none of my friends had expected the reunion they were given.

Surrounded by moss and long green vines, Juniper slept with her eyes gently closed. Her skin was pale and her dress was torn, but an intricate wildflower crown wove around the top of her golden-brown hair. The droplet faeries had gathered beside her arms.

My heart felt like it had dropped into the depths of my spirit. I thought about the tragic possibility of the girl's death. Nevertheless, each of us quickly took notice of the steady rise and fall of her chest.

"She's alive," Ronan whispered.

"We need to get her back to the Academy." Violet looked up at me with tear-streaked eyes and panic in her voice.

A billion thoughts were running through my mind. What were we going to do? How could we possibly get Juniper back to the castle while she was unconscious? I thought about carrying her, but decided it would take far too long and we would be exhausted by the time we reached the stream.

A sudden gust of wind came blowing through the trees, and I glanced over at Ariadne to see a tiny smile on her face. Her hands were raised toward the sky as tears streamed down her cheeks.

"Ariadne, would you *please* stop doing that?"

The unfamiliar voice caused me to jump. Juniper's eyelids flickered, and her nose twitched with the over-whelming perfume of flowers. I looked down just in time to witness the opening of her wide emerald gaze.

"Juniper," Violet whispered. "You're alive!"

CHAPTER NINETEEN

"Where am I?" Juniper asked as the droplet faeries climbed across her freckled shoulders.

"Those tiny creatures have been tending to her ever since she appeared," Willoughby told us. "I've been living in this forest for nearly a hundred years, but ye don't see them treating me like royalty!"

Ariadne and Violet swung their arms around Juniper, while I stood back and observed the interaction. Ariadne's Gift had awoken the last Elemental. A few moments ago, it had seemed as though such a thing were impossible.

Juniper lifted her hand to her head. Her eyes were filled with the faded morning stars and nearly a thousand unreadable emotions. I watched as each of the memories began to flood back into her eyes, while she examined our faces with a thoughtful expression. The wild-haired girl knew neither of the Hanley sisters, although she seemed familiar.

❧❧❧❧

Not long after Juniper had awoken, we decided to make our way back to the castle. The dry earth crunched beneath my boots as we crossed over the meadow of wildflowers. Whilst carefully eyeing the ground for any tiny people, I felt a tap on my shoulder. I glanced over to see Ariadne and Juniper striding behind me.

"These girls are Alice and Emery Hanley," Ariadne introduced us to her friend. "If it weren't for the two of them, I'm not sure we would have found you."

"This may sound a bit odd, but I feel like I already know you," Juniper told us. "Are you sure we have not met before?"

"I'm quite sure," said Emery. "This is our first year at the Academy for Gifted Youth, and we do not live in the realm of Aisling."

"Well, then you are quite right," Juniper laughed. "I have never left this realm, but my feet have walked in many lands."

❧❧❧❧

When we finally returned to the castle, it was nearly four o'clock in the morning. I expected the school to be in a state of turmoil as they searched for five missing students. However, the castle was silent. The only sound was the distant noise of the gardeners working in the courtyard.

I suppose none of us had any lingering concern about getting caught, for together we ran up the steps and through the towering castle doors. The entrance hall was silent; not a voice or footstep could be heard.

"We must take her to the headmistress," Ronan whispered.

Every word echoed throughout the corridors, and I cringed with the hope that no one heard us. We each nodded before hurrying across the entrance hall and ascending the white stairwell. As we traveled upward, the light from every window shone brightly across the castle walls, and the morning sun rose steadily above the trees.

Emery and I led the group down the candlelit passage. We wove our way through the silent halls until we stood just outside the sparkling door to Zara's office. I almost expected the entrance to swing open with rage, but the moment never came. Before I had the chance to knock, the door began to creak open. The six of us peered quietly around the corner to see the headmistress watching us from the comfort of her desk.

"It's very nice to have you back," she spoke with a voice as smooth as glass.

"How did you know we were gone?" asked Ariadne.

"I suppose it may have been a wise decision to bring Kade O'Reilly with you on this daring quest," Zara stated flatly. "Perhaps she would not have awoken to find all three of her roommates missing from the castle."

My eyes dropped to the floor. I had completely forgotten about Kade. I knew she would feel terribly betrayed.

"You're not angry?" Ronan asked.

"I'm not angry, Ronan," she responded. "However, I do feel a bit surprised. I assumed one of you would have told me about this idea, without sneaking out in the middle of the night. You very well could have been killed."

We stood in the middle of the room as the young woman folded her hands neatly on the desk in front of her. Her expression changed a bit as her eyes met those of Juniper Stone.

"Nevertheless, I appreciate the courage it took for Ronan and Violet to follow the three of you on this daring quest. I'm very glad to see Juniper with us today."

A small grin appeared on Juniper's freckled face. Despite her torn dress and the bramble scratches across her limbs, the last elemental appeared to be brave. After everything each of us had experienced, I knew our actions were heroic.

"Ronan and Violet, you are dismissed," Zara sighed.

I watched quietly as our friends glanced at us with an expression of confusion. After a moment of silence, they continued to walk through the door. I knew what this was about. The headmistress was simply waiting to speak about the prophecy.

"You are welcome to find a seat." Zara gestured to the four chairs that had suddenly appeared in front of her desk.

I placed myself in the middle with Emery, while Juniper and Ariadne seated themselves on either side of us. My gaze wandered around the shelves of books and potions, which lined every corner of the office. The dawn light was just beginning to peer through the beautiful glass windows.

"I want to speak to the four of you, personally," the headmistress began. "What you did last night was very heroic. Although I may be upset you failed to inform me, I must admit I'm grateful for your actions."

The four of us glanced at each other in silence. I had not expected such a reaction from the headmistress.

"Juniper," Zara addressed the untidy girl. "I know it has only been a short time since you've been back, but I must ask if there is anything you remember from the attack."

My gaze shifted in the direction of Violet's cousin, who tucked a strand of curly hair behind her left ear.

"It was dawn," Juniper spoke as her face lost all expression. "Sunrise had passed, and we were making our way through the Night Oak Forest. I was enjoying the view from the carriage window and listening to the clatter of hooves on the path. We eventually came to a sudden stop."

Emery shifted uncomfortably in her seat. A strange expression settled upon the surface of her cerulean eyes. My sister despised scary stories.

128

"The carriage was beginning to bounce, and the horses were becoming unsettled," Juniper explained. "I poked my head out the window, although I did not see anything wrong. I called out to the coachman, but his response was unheard. That is the last moment I remember before waking up in the White Birch Forest."

The room was silent for a minute. The headmistress was staring at the four of us with a thoughtful expression. "I wonder how it is that you awoke in an entirely different place than where you were attacked."

"I'm not quite sure," Juniper said slowly. "The entire ordeal is a bit of a haze now."

"I've been waiting over fifteen years for the four of you to be standing together in the Academy for Gifted Youth," Zara sighed. "I don't think I ever realized that simply having you together is not enough. The prophecy needs to be fulfilled in a way I have yet to understand. I have tried everything, but it is now up to the four of you."

"How are *we* supposed to figure this out? You cannot expect us to complete a prophecy we discovered only a month ago," Ariadne started. Nevertheless, each of us knew Juniper had been told about the prophecy many years ago.

"You must find the courage to work together. The ancient prophecy never stated Zara Hawthorne would be the one to save the realm of Aisling from destruction," the headmistress reminded us. "This prophecy is about the four of you."

CHAPTER TWENTY

The return of Juniper was quite discreet. Zara made no indication that the girl had returned; however, she had not announced a disappearance either. Everyone had known she was gone, and everyone seemed to marvel at her return.

The four of us visited the library that afternoon. As we came back through the door of Lancaster Hall, we were greeted by an explosion of cheers. My eyes wandered through a large crowd of friends. Everyone had been crowned in flowers, and garlands decorated the railing of the library loft. It took me a moment to realize this gathering was a celebration of our sixteenth birthday.

An excited squeal came from the loft above us. I glanced up to see Augusta standing at the foot of the ladder. Her curly brown hair bounced with glee as she hurried down the steps.

"Happy birthday!" she exclaimed before gathering the four of us in a tight group hug.

The rest of the girls crowned us in flowers and handed us our gifts. We each settled on the floor of the library loft. The whole of Lancaster Hall was alive with music and laughter. Augusta presented me with an official Aisling compass, while my sister opened a very intricate map of the realm. I smiled before sticking the compass in my coat pocket.

Kade avoided us during the majority of the party. She was upset to learn we had forgotten to include her in our adventure. I hoped she would forgive our thoughtless actions.

The party went on until Augusta sent each of us back to our chambers. Although I had been enjoying myself, I was quite delighted to have a moment alone. It seemed as though my sixteenth birthday had flown by in a matter of minutes, yet my shoulders felt tired under the weight of our adventurous activity. I never had the chance to open my vial necklace.

I watched as the glimmering moonlight shone brightly through our bedroom window. The only other source of light was the flickering candle at my bedside. Once everyone had fallen asleep, I ignited a flame in the palm of my left hand. I reached into the collar of my nightgown and pulled out the old glass vial. My heart skipped a beat with the anticipation of finally discovering the contents of the mysterious necklace.

Opening the vial was much harder than I expected. After placing the little cork on my bedside table, the note fell out into my other hand. I marveled at the old piece of paper for a moment before carefully unfolding the note. The writing was so attentive that I thought it would be best to call it calligraphy.

Four towers stand tall in the evening light,
as each reflect an element in sight.

Do not misjudge the creatures of the night,
for they shall not give up without a fight.

With fire in her hair and flames in her eyes,
she shall see how the elements will rise.

My eyes ran over the piece of prose several times before I stopped to think. It seemed as if my late grandmother had known about the prophecy. Every written word reminded me of the page in Zara's library book.

As my sister began to snore, I quickly stuck the note back into the vial. I tucked the necklace back into the collar of my shirt and closed my eyes. My mind was filled with questions I knew could never be answered. I searched through every memory of my remarkable grandmother, although nothing seemed to explain the letter she had left in her wake.

CHAPTER TWENTY-ONE

As the month of December arrived, each of the students were sent home for three weeks of winter break. I was acclimated to the warm weather of Aisling; therefore, heading back to New England was a bit of a climate change. Winter lasted for a very short period of time in the realm of Aisling. I cherished this magical weather, for the flowers never seemed to die and the meadows seldom turned to gray. White frost collected on the pink rosebushes, and my sister rejoiced in the presence of the first snow.

Returning to my family was a marvelous experience. I personally believe our horses were just as excited to go riding as we were, for nothing could outshine our gleeful trail rides in the snow. On Christmas morning, our father baked his famous cookies, and my family opened presents around the fire. I realized I had grown numb to my longing for home. Homesickness only lasted for the first couple of weeks at school, but my heart always missed the essence of our household. Aisling held a new place in my heart. In time, the Gifted realm would be just as much of a home as the old white farmhouse.

Winter break felt as though it passed just as quickly as it came. I wondered if our mother would ever let us return to Aisling, for her brown eyes seemed to sparkle whenever we walked through the door. It pained me to see her light fade as we stood before the portal once more. Nevertheless, we had a prophecy to complete. The people of Aisling were depending on the Four Elementals. As I stepped through Violet's enchanted portal, I made a promise that I would never let them down.

After we returned to the Academy, our time quickly became filled with assignments from the professors. Despite the heavy pile of schoolwork, my mind was focused on the note in my vial necklace.

I tried to find peace in the library, but the students crowded every corner. Despite the constant scolding from the elderly librarian, the voices eventually grew too loud for me to think. I shoved the thick stack of textbooks into my messenger bag and hurried through the door.

A moment after I stepped into the hallway, a familiar voice called my name. I glanced over my shoulder to see Violet running after me. Her eyes were bright with laughter, and a book bag swung heavily in her right arm.

"Hello," I greeted my friend as she slowed down beside me.

"I owe you quite a debt, Alice. Without you and your sister, I do not know that Juniper would be with us today. You should have seen the joyful faces upon her family this Christmas," Violet told me. "I never found the chance to express my gratitude."

I watched as she fought back a stream of iridescent tears. I did consider myself responsible for the discovery of Juniper Stone. Without the Gifts of Violet and Ariadne, I was sure we never would have found the last elemental.

"No act of kindness deserves a debt in return," I responded with a smile. "I owe you just as much as you owe me."

When I reached the end of the hallway, I glanced toward the towering grandfather clock that swung gracefully in front of Ruby Lane's office. It was nearly time for lunch, yet not one of my assignments had been completed. My stomach felt as though it were about to collapse with hunger. My feet hurried down the stairwell and toward the crowded dining hall.

I glanced around before strolling along the line of tables. Scanning for an empty chair, I discovered a seat across from Ronan and Kade. My sister was nowhere to be found, but I assumed she was probably eating lunch within the courtyard.

"Good afternoon, Alice!" Ronan greeted me, before discreetly encouraging his sister to do the same.

Kade glanced up from her book without saying a word. It quickly became apparent that she was still ignoring my presence. Ronan watched me with the clearest bit of hope that I would not take it personally. My gut twisted with the guilt of forgetting to share the information of our quest to find Juniper, but I also felt a stab of anger toward my winged friend. She was skilled at the art of holding a grudge.

I stood up from my chair and swung my bag over my shoulder. After grabbing a lionberry scone from my plate, I hurried back down the line of tables. As I pushed open the heavy doors, I decided to apologize to Kade in the future. If she did not forgive me, there was nothing more to do. My friend was acting childish, but I was beginning to hope time was not the only thing that could heal such wounds.

My boots tapped against the smooth floor of the entrance hall before I pushed open the castle door and hurried down the front steps. If my friends knew the truth, I was sure they would understand. Neither Kade nor Ronan had any idea about the prophecy. My hair began to spark with madness, and I allowed each strand to go up in flames.

I wasn't sure I had any idea where I was going, but I allowed my footsteps to lead me into the unknown. After a moment, I was standing at the base of one of the

Four Lone Towers. I had heard the legends about these buildings, which had been locked for over a century. No person had been able to open the tower doors since the days of the Academy founder. Nevertheless, it took a moment for this to dawn on me as I grasped the handle, and the heavy door swung open with a creak.

I stood in disbelief, glancing around to make sure I was alone. The only sound was the distant bit of laughter that came from the flickering golden light of the dining hall windows. A spiraling staircase stood inside the open doorway, reaching toward the sky. The air was dusty, and countless cobwebs lined the walls, but I took a deep breath before stepping inside.

Almost unconscious of my own actions, I ignited the pair of torches that hung on either side of the entrance. As I began to ascend the stairwell, my fire guided the path of curiosity. The tower was completely dark, despite the occasional stream of light shining brightly across the shadowed steps. The stairs seemed to last for eternity, although this changed when I came to a halt at the top of the building.

A familiar wooden door stood before me. I gasped with the sudden realization that it was a mirror image of the one upon my wardrobe in the castle. My fingers ran softly along the engravings before I jumped back. A tiny flame had leaped from my fingertips, transforming into a stream of golden light that traveled quickly across the grooves. I watched in wonder as the entire door became illuminated in a flaming trail.

The tower echoed as the passage began to unlock. After grabbing the crystal handle, I pushed open the door. Despite the sunlight that streamed through the stone balcony, the top of the tower was almost completely dark. As my flames illuminated several torches along the ancient walls, the room began to grow a little brighter. The tower seemed to bring the rest of the world into view, and the only limits were found on the distant horizon.

As I dropped my book bag on the floor, textbooks fell out across the stone. I took a bite of my scone before pulling out an old sketchbook. All thoughts of schoolwork abandoned, I flipped to a clean page and began to draw out a map of the Academy grounds. I spent several hours on this project, glancing up occasionally to gaze upon the spectacular view.

When I was in the middle of sketching out the Droplet Meadow, a sudden thought occurred to me. I reached into the collar of my shirt and pulled out the old vial necklace. The cork popped off much easier this time, and I proceeded to unfold the note in my hand.

Four towers stand tall in the evening light,
As each reflect an element in sight.

I was finally beginning to piece the words together. After closing my sketchbook and grabbing my messenger bag, I hurried back through the door. I flicked my wrist to extinguish the flames, leaving the tower just as it had been found. My mind was racing as I reached the end of the spiral stairwell.

Peeking through a tiny crack in the door, I noticed a few of my fellow students wandering quietly down the gravel path. After deciding it was safe to leave, I hurried through the door. Trying not to look suspicious, I trotted up the dew-covered slope and onto the path before me. My legs swung with swift and ungraceful strides.

Following the path that led toward the courtyard, I swung open the vine-covered gate. Juniper, Ariadne, and Emery were seated at one of the old tea tables. As I walked between the vibrant flowers, it came to my attention that my friends were already engrossed in serious conversation.

"Good afternoon, Alice," Juniper greeted me with a smile.

I came to a halt in front of the last empty chair. Emery and Ariadne looked up at me with careful expressions. I knew something important had occurred. Emery glanced at the other two girls with hesitation before she spoke.

"Something very peculiar has happened," my sister whispered in a small voice.

My gaze wandered curiously around the garden, looking for some sort of an explanation. Nothing appeared to be out of place. I looked back at my sister with an expression of confusion.

"Take my hand," Emery told me. Her piercing eyes penetrated through me in a way I had never seen before. My sister was not commanding me to do anything, but she was asking me to place my trust in her hands.

As I rested my hand on her ice-cold palm, some-thing dramatically changed. The wind began to swirl furiously around us, uprooting the garden soil in a dusty haze. The tips of my ginger hair began to spark. The colors of our surroundings began to disappear as my vision swirled into an empty darkness.

The shadows were merely momentary. My amber eyes opened wide as a burst of light and extraordinary color came into view. For a long moment, I believed I had entered a dream. Sudden and familiar memories appeared before me like a screenplay. They came in fleeting glimpses, but I managed to capture every one.

I was standing in the middle of a sunlit room. No one seemed to notice my presence, but my eyes quickly fo-cused on two unmistakably familiar faces from across the room. A little girl with curly red hair stood beside a large vase of sunflowers. She was accompanied by another young girl, who looked remarkably similar to my twin sister. Their laughter echoed in my ears, as though it were something the human mind was unable to comprehend.

I did not understand the purpose of traveling back to this memory. Almost every recent event was connected to the prophecy in one way or another. I was quite confident that this memory held the same importance.

As if to call upon my suspicions, the heavy vase fell suddenly to the floor, spilling water and golden petals across the wood. I barely had enough time to think before my vision spiraled into darkness once more.

Only a moment after they had closed, my eyelids opened to the bright light of new surroundings. I was standing on the front steps of an old stone cottage in the middle of an Aisling village. A dusty-haired woman was hurrying down the cobblestone road. Her balance teetered back and forth under the weight of two heavy baskets, which had been piled high with novels of every sort.

A young girl trailed behind her, skipping through the autumn leaves as her short brown hair blew wildly in the breeze. With every step the young girl took, a trail of miniature wind spirals twirled in her wake. Each footstep swept away the fallen leaves in a curious golden vortex. Her lightly freckled face was home to a pixie-like nose and familiar pair of gray eyes.

"Hurry up, Ariadne! We mustn't be late!" The woman's voice echoed throughout my mind before I blinked myself into another peculiar scene.

I was standing in front of another stone cottage. Its vine-covered gate and cobblestone wall traveled down an old dirt road for as far as the eye could see. In the faint distance, the meadow grass danced in the breeze as curious songbirds swept through the trees. I stood for a short moment, listening to their song, until the familiar sound of horseshoes began to beat down the path.

After turning my head, I noticed a figure cantering toward me. The rider was a young girl with sparkling emerald eyes and a mess of curly, golden hair. Her face was slightly younger, and her hair was slightly shorter, but I had no doubt in my mind that she was Juniper Stone.

Her noble steed was oblivious to my presence as he came to a halt in front of the cottage. His gentle brown eyes looked past me with an uninterested expression, while Juniper slid out of the saddle and swung open the gate. I followed her and the old gelding through the grass until we reached a large paddock near the other side of the house. After leading her horse inside, Juniper quickly pulled off his tack and gave him a gentle grooming. The dappled gelding stood quietly as I watched the dust sweep from his coat with every gentle stroke.

"Juniper, where are you?" I heard a woman call from the direction of the house.

"I'll be right there," Juniper called back before placing her brush on the old stone wall and glancing back at her horse. "I'll be back in just a moment, Sampson."

As Juniper ran toward the house, I watched helplessly as the paddock gate escaped the grasp of the lock. The old steed did not seem to notice, but I was sure the autumn breeze would swing the gate open. Juniper would come back to discover her horse was gone.

Out of the corner of my eye, I noticed something move. The tangled mess of vines that grew wild on the gate had begun to weave their way around the wooden

142

fence. Reaching out like a hand, the agile plant began to pull the paddock gate into its keeper. A bright light clouded my vision, leading me to our final destination.

CHAPTER TWENTY-TWO

I stood at the foot of a small staircase in the hallway of my old home. I suppose one might say that things looked only slightly different. The kitchen door was a cozy shade of plum, instead of the brilliant blue my sister had convinced our father to paint it just a few years ago. A different basket held the umbrellas, and the coatrack was not quite the same. However, when I looked up, I could still see the giant oil painting that hung above the stairwell.

As I walked around the corner and into my family's kitchen, I was greeted by a high-pitched scream. The moment I had stepped through the doorway, every light in our white farmhouse vanished. As I gazed through the darkness, my vision could just barely distinguish between the silhouettes of two little girls.

I do not believe anyone understands the definition of the word "surreal" until they experienced it. Between the sight of my ginger curls gleaming in the moonlight and the sound of my sister's unmistakable voice, nothing seemed stranger than seeing my face as more than a photograph or mirror reflection.

"The candles are in the cabinet under the silverware." I turned around to see my mother standing in the doorway, holding a flashlight in her right hand. The ray of light shone upon the two young faces, as though the children were a pair of lost travelers. We must have been no more than eight years old, although my hair was just as red.

Giggles filled the air as the two figures ran around the kitchen table. They swung the cabinet doors open and lifted out a heavy little box, which I knew to be filled with our mother's favorite scented candles.

Mom walked over and lifted the box off the floor before setting it down on the table. She opened the lid and pulled out the first candle she could find. "By the time we are done, the entire house will smell like… Christmas cookies!" She laughed after pausing to read the label.

"That's my favorite!" I heard a tiny voice and glanced down to see I was standing beside my younger self. Just like the noble steed, her amber eyes were completely oblivious to my presence. My body was still in the courtyard garden, and this experience was nothing more than a dream.

A few moments later, the girls began to distribute candles all around the house. Our mother followed with a box of matches. I made my way into the living room, allowing my skin to soak in the candlelight. Despite it being the middle of springtime, I enjoyed the fresh smell of Christmas cookies and the essence of this memory.

After a moment, something remarkable happened. My eyes just barely caught it, but I watched in fascination as my eight-year-old body placed a candle in the center of the room and turned away just in time to miss the flame that appeared inside. I whipped my head around to see if our mother had been watching, but she was busy lighting the line of candles along the mantelpiece.

It seemed like no more than the blink of an eye before I found myself standing in the courtyard. Every one of my senses came back in a rush as the scent of flowers overwhelmed me into a sneeze. I looked up to see Juniper, Ariadne, and Emery watching me with strange expressions of curiosity.

"This isn't normal," I whispered, slumping back into my chair.

"I think we've covered that," remarked Ariadne.

"I don't believe this is about us being normal," Juniper said. "We already know we are quite far from ordinary. Normality is much less captivating than the extraordinary."

"Perhaps this is about us being different," Emery added. "Everyone is born with a destiny and purpose. The prophecy could be one of ours."

I nodded in agreement, for my sister was right. My favorite part of Aisling was the fact that every person had been taught to see the beauty in each other. No one had questioned this teaching since the days of Silas Casper and Wolfgang Gregory; however, the curse threatened to bring a terrible change. The prophecy was an important part of our fate. We simply needed to follow our destiny.

I found myself wondering if I should tell my friends about the Four Lone Towers. The prophecy seemed to be unfolding faster than I expected. Unexplainable hesitation and uncertainty lingered in the shadows of my mind.

"I have something to show you," I told them quietly as I stepped out of my chair.

My sister looked up at me with confusion. We never kept secrets from each other, and we always trusted each other to keep a secret. Nevertheless, this was the reason why I chose to share the truth.

My friends followed me out of the garden. The castle grounds appeared to be deserted, and the only sound was the crunch of gravel beneath our shoes. We hurried down the dew-soaked hillside and toward the old stone tower. Once we reached the wooden door, I turned to face my Gifted friends.

"You each know the story of these four towers," I affirmed. "They have been locked without a key for over a century. No one has been able to open the doors since the founder of the Academy."

"This cannot be possible," Juniper gasped as I placed my hand on the knob and the door swung open with a creak.

"Somebody must have unlocked it," Ariadne said as she glanced around to make sure nobody else was watching. "I'm sure you're not the only one who has been able to open it."

I thought about this for a moment. The headmistress may have finally figured out a way to break into the towers without destroying them. It was possible she had left the door unlocked, although I was not going to settle upon this idea without evidence.

I swung the door shut before gesturing for Ariadne to try it. She stepped forward until she was standing at the foot of the tower, and she placed her delicate hand around the silver doorknob. I heard the clicking sound of a lock as she turned it sideways, and the door refused to open. Ariadne gave me a strange look before trying the handle once more. But I knew I was right. The tower was locked. I was the only person who had been able to open the door in over a century.

I glanced at my sister. Her pale eyebrows furrowed into a thoughtful expression.

"What is it, Emery?" Juniper asked before I had the chance to do the same.

"I'm just thinking," Emery responded with a quiet voice. "There are four towers, correct?"

"Yes." I nodded as we made our way back up the hill and toward the castle steps.

"There are four of us as well." She lowered her voice as we passed a group of younger students. They were too busy laughing at each other to hear anything we had to say.

"I have a feeling each of the towers belongs to one of us," Emery said as soon as the other students were out of earshot.

"Perhaps Ariadne was not able to open this tower, because it does not belong to her," concluded Juniper.

Emery nodded as we hurried up the castle steps and came to a halt in front of the door. There was a brief pause in the conversation as I pulled my necklace out of my collar. My sister's eyes widened with surprise.

"You still have that old thing?" she gasped. "I thought you would have opened it ages ago."

"I saved it until our sixteenth birthday," I explained, before slipping the note into my hand and passing it around to each of them. "I don't know how our grandmother knew about the prophecy, but this letter confirms everything we have been wondering."

I watched each of their expressions change as they examined the elegant handwriting. The silence seemed to echo through my ears, as though it were begging our voices to speak. Nevertheless, words did not seem necessary.

CHAPTER TWENTY-THREE

The next few days were unusually quiet. I avoided all interactions as I hurried down the castle corridors. My mind was comparable to the afternoon sky, clouded with ideas and the occasional concern, which popped into my head like a bird soaring through a never-ending sea of blue.

I was not sure why I had entered the library, although my thoughts were often organized between the enchanting bookshelves. Skimming through the history aisle, I found myself face-to-face with a collection of books dedicated to the Four Lone Towers. I reached out and pulled a volume from the shelf.

A few of our professors had mentioned the towers in class; however, they never spoke about the structures in much detail. I always assumed this was because the Academy preferred to keep the students away from the ancient doors. Even so, as the prophecy was beginning to unfold, the concern was understandable.

I gathered more of the books into a pile and carried them over to the librarian's desk. A familiar boy stood behind the counter with his back toward me. His curly brown hair and green wool sweater seemed well acquainted to my amber eyes. As he turned around, I recognized a very familiar face of freckles.

"Hello, Alice," Ronan greeted me with an expression of surprise.

"Ronan, what are you doing here?" I asked.

"I thought Kade already told you," he responded awkwardly. "I started working here last weekend. The librarian was searching for volunteers."

"Oh." I nodded, dropping the heavy pile of books in front of him.

"Is there a new assignment of which I am unaware?" the boy asked suspiciously as his blue eyes rested on each of the bindings.

"I've just decided to do a bit of extra studying." I attempted to think of a valid excuse for such a curious history topic.

"You hate studying," Ronan reminded me as he began to check out each of the books.

"I do not!" I retorted.

"Yes, you do!" Ronan laughed. "You told me just the other day when we were in class with my uncle."

"There isn't any extra homework," I said firmly. "I'm doing this for myself."

"All right," Ronan spoke with a tone of suspicion. He watched as I gathered the books in my arms and headed for the door.

"Alice," the boy called. "Please do not take Kade personally. She may be upset with you now, but she will forget about the matter in a few days.

I nodded with the slightest bit of a smile before walking down the spiral staircase. Ronan was trying to ease the tension between his sister and me, but I highly doubted that Kade would be over our feud so quickly. Grudges are often worse enemies than pain.

When I arrived in my room, it was almost time for dinner. My shoulders felt heavy under the weight of my books, and I barely made it into the bedroom before dropping them on the surface of my mattress. The other girls had already made their way to the dining hall.

After a few minutes, I heard a soft knock and looked up to see Augusta standing in the doorway. Her curly brown hair was tied into a messy bun, and her wide-framed glasses rested gently on the bridge of her nose.

"It seems like the rest of Lancaster Hall has already made their way down to the dining hall," she announced. "Would you care to join me?"

I nodded with a smile.

As we wandered through the castle, neither of us spoke a word. I found comfort in the presence of another quiet spirit. My heart found solitude in the tranquility of silence, for those were the rare moments when I was able to lose myself in the freedom of my surroundings.

Upon entering the dining hall, I found a seat beside the other Elementals. The room was bursting with laughter and conversation from our fellow students; however, the three of us ate our food in silence.

Juniper stared blankly across the dining hall as she took a bite out of a plump lionberry. Her emerald eyes held an unreadable expression as they wandered through the crowd of students. There was no doubt the attack was still haunting her mind.

"What will each of you be doing this summer?" I asked, feeling the need to break the unnerving silence that lingered in our corner of the hall. It was barely the middle of February, although the seasons of Aisling changed much faster than they did in my old world. Springtime would be ending soon, and the semester was drawing to a close.

"I'll probably be working at the Moss Shop." Ariadne sighed heavily.

"Not if I can help it!" Juniper laughed.

I envied the two of them, for they had both grown up in the realm of Aisling. I found myself wondering what it would be like to stay for just the summer. After gulping down the last spoonful of soup, I grabbed a lionberry from one of the fruit baskets and stood up from my chair.

"Where are you going, Alice?" inquired Emery.

"I'm not feeling very well," I responded. "I think I'll head back to the dormitories."

Truthfully, I was feeling fine. I simply could not keep my focus on the conversation with my friends.

My mind was racing with curiosity for the towers and our prophecy.

As my feet carried me through the dining hall doors, I nearly collided with Zara Hawthorne. Her sapphire eyes did not seem fazed. I bowed my head apologetically.

"Good evening, Alice," Zara greeted me. "Are you leaving dinner already?"

"Uh… yes," I responded with an awkward pause. "I'm afraid I have some extra studying to finish."

"I saw you in the library this afternoon," she responded with a brief nod. "You appeared to be leaving with a great number of books."

The headmistress was beginning to make me feel self-conscious, but it was evident that her pursed lips were holding back a grin. Zara hoped I was beginning to decode the prophecy.

"You know, Alice," she continued in a hushed tone of voice. "When one finds themselves with the task of solving a challenging puzzle, the best way to understand the solution is to avoid overthinking."

I remained silent. The headmistress was remarkably good at reading people. She had noticed my wandering focus and pensive gaze.

"You must trust yourself, Alice," said Zara. "When the time comes, I believe your heart will know its task and your spirit shall guide you to your destiny."

Zara seemed to speak in her own prophecy. Her wisdom often caused me to forget about her young age. I admired the advice she gave to others, and the simple way words flowed from her like poetry when one needed it most. I had no doubt this was one of the many reasons Zara had been chosen as the headmistress of the Academy for Gifted Youth.

I stood before the entrance of Lancaster Hall, reaching out to place my hand where the doorknob might have been. I thought back to my very first day at the Academy for Gifted Youth and realized it was not so long ago. The time passed with swift strides, and it didn't care enough to give notice. I had made several extraordinary friends, and the prophecy was keeping my thoughts busy.

I closed the door behind me and hurried through the lounge. After grabbing one of the books from my bed-chamber, I climbed the sturdy ladder of the loft. The old hardcover was coated in dust and silver lettering. As my fingers trailed down the inky pages, each separate word danced gracefully in my mind.

The Four Lone Towers are one of the most famous mysteries in all of Aisling. They are the trademark of the Academy for Gifted Youth, which is settled in the lush, green valley that many know to be the barrier of the Night Oak and White Birch Forests. Each tower was built shortly after the castle of the Academy for Gifted Youth.

The founder of the Academy, Professor Silas Casper, spent much of his time in each of the four towers. It was there he studied art, literature, astronomy, and magical Gifts.

Boredom began to linger in the back of my mind. The library books did not seem to hold any additional information about the prophecy. As I glanced down, two individual flames kindled in the palm of my hand. I watched carefully as they dashed down my line of fingers and leaped into the air with freedom. I smiled with the knowledge that these flames would always be a reflection of my soul.

Professor Hawthorne's words were true. I did not need to drive myself mad with the objective of comprehension. Fate intertwines with everyday life, even when people fail to pay attention. Such a truth is comparable to the art of climbing mountains; the struggle is greatest before you reach the summit.

CHAPTER TWENTY-FOUR

Several days later, dust began to collect upon the old hardcovers. I decided to return the books to the Academy library, as there was no use in allowing them to sit any longer.

"I will be back in a few minutes," I called to my sister, who sat cross-legged on her bed. She nodded without taking her eyes away from the novel in her hands. I watched for a moment as her blue gaze traveled quickly down the lines of ink.

As I hurried down the hallway, my shoulders began to feel the weight of the heavy books gathered in my arms. I adjusted the pile every few minutes, quickening my pace in an attempt to reach the library sooner. The castle appeared to be deserted; however, a familiar face appeared as I rounded the corner beside the stairwell.

"Can I help you?" Ronan smiled at me behind the mountain of books.

I remained silent for a moment, contemplating my few options. My friend did not wait for a response, as he removed half of the volumes from the stack. Without a word, we sauntered down the wooden stairwell. The morning light shone through the castle windows, leaving each step with the reflection of faded colors. The hallway echoed with the sound of footsteps, breaking the silence with every reverberation.

"Something fascinating occurred to me yesterday," said Ronan.

"What was it?" I asked, attempting to keep the silence from creeping back in.

"There are four elementally Gifted students in the Academy at the same time. Each of you share the same birthday," stated Ronan. "Isn't that odd? After all, the four elements are very rare Gifts."

As I watched him, my heart pounded like a drum in my chest. Ronan was beginning to discern my secret. I always assumed Zara intended to keep the prophecy unknown, though I did not know what would happen if the truth began to leak out.

"I'm sure you have thought about it, as the four of you are such close friends," Ronan continued as he became conscious of my stare. "I just thought it seemed a bit strange."

"I'm sure it is just a coincidence." I laughed, opening my hand to reveal a bright orange flame.

❧❦❦❧

I sat with the other girls at lunch in the afternoon. The world seemed to fade into a blur of colors as I became lost in the forest of my mind. The past few days seemed like pieces in a never-ending puzzle. The prophecy was beginning to remind me of a broken camera. The lens would come into focus at certain times, but everything seemed to blur in the moment when I needed clarity.

Violet and Kade rushed toward us as we stood up from our chairs. I wondered if they were purposely late for lunch or simply lost track of time. Either way, relief washed over Kade's face, as she was waiting for us to leave the table.

"You must have arrived early," Violet laughed as though she weren't late.

As we left the dining hall, the eyes of our friends bore through the back of our necks, like poison seeping through the skin. They were full of suspicion and wonder, which I had grown to recognize as two very dangerous things. The voices of our classmates were deafening. As we stepped outside the castle walls, the shelter of nature seemed to hold its hands over my ears.

"What is the plan, Alice?" Ariadne questioned.

"Follow me."

After a synchronized nod from each of them, my friends followed me around the side of the castle. The air was silent. The majority of the students had been wary of leaving the castle since the day of Juniper's disappearance. The Night Oak Forest appeared to be very welcoming in the daylight, although we each knew better than to stray down the shadowed path.

Once we reached the edge of the presentation meadow, I gestured to one of the Four Lone Towers in the distance. The other girls gave an occasional sigh and groan of irritation as we trekked across the vast acreage. The wind buffeted strongly against the ancient tower walls, and our hair blew wildly through the air as the four of us gathered silently near the old tower doorstep.

"Why don't you give it a try?" Juniper prompted my sister.

After a moment, Emery wrapped her snow-white fingers around the doorknob. As she turned the handle, it refused to open. A faint trace of frost leaped from her skin, swirling across the useless keyhole. My sister stepped back with a small expression of disappointment.

Ariadne glanced at me with hesitation before turning the old doorknob. I heard the familiar clicking sound of a lock before the entrance swung open with the wind. The girl stared through the doorway with an expression of astonishment. My friends wanted nothing more than to explore the interior of their towers; however, we knew such an adventure would have to wait.

Juniper's tower rested near the other corner of the White Birch Forest. Its vine-covered walls faded away into the clouded sky. Beneath every bit of green, a tiny pink flower was hidden amongst the stones. The door swung open on the first attempt.

On the other side of the castle grounds, my sister's tower stood almost directly across from mine. A small creek babbled near its base, and sunlight dappled beneath the shadowed waters. With a radiant smile on her face, my sister opened the unbreakable door.

❧❦❧❦

As the four of us ate our dinner, we each contributed a piece of artwork to my new map of the Academy grounds. We did not mention the towers or speak a word of the prophecy until the meal was finished. The castle was far too busy, and we were sure to be overheard.

As Emery placed her hand over a steaming cup of peppermint tea, the silence seemed to envelop the room. All conversations died down. My sister must have grown distracted, as her cup of tea eventually iced over. Her blue eyes stared past me with an unreadable expression.

Glancing over my shoulder, I caught sight of the headmistress standing in the doorway. She was accompanied by a rugged-looking man. His shaggy brown hair looked desperate for a shower, and his boots were equally as dirty. Across his shoulder was an arrow quiver; he held a longbow in his right hand.

After a long moment, they strode across the floor, toward the center of the room. I assumed there was going to be an announcement; however, my suspicions were wrong. Zara hurried directly toward my table and placed her strong hand around my shoulder.

"Alice," she whispered urgently. "Gather your friends and meet me in the entrance hall."

Her sapphire eyes bore through me with an expression I had never seen before. Her face held a distinct look of urgency and dread. Something was very wrong, and the headmistress did not dare announce it to the entire school. Her gaze darted around the room, unable to settle on the character of a single student.

I nodded without question.

As the headmistress hurried back through the doorway, Emery glanced down at her frozen cup of tea. Reaching across the table, I tapped one finger on the ice, and the tea melted back into a liquid form. Gathering her novel and steaming teacup, Emery followed me toward the entrance hall.

Juniper and Ariadne greeted us beside the doorway. They seemed confused, anxious, and slightly concerned. It was evident that each of us had experienced the apprehension that gathered in the back of my mind. We stepped through the heavy doors and into the marble hall. Beside the castle windows, Zara was pacing back and forth. The archer stood beside the stairwell, examining the feathers on each of his arrows.

"What is going on?" Ariadne inquired.

"This is Lachlan. He is one of the head archers for the Guardians of Aisling," Zara explained as she gestured to the man beside her. "He has come to inform us that four of the Academy students have been targeted by the Creatures of the Night Oak Forest."

Juniper and I exchanged a look of uncertainty before shifting our gazes toward the archer. Despite his appearance, Lachlan seemed trustworthy. Nevertheless, we could not be certain.

"The Guardians of Aisling know everything about the prophecy." Zara waved her hand to dismiss our concerns. "It is part of their job to protect you."

"The Creatures of the Night Oak Forest know you are here. They have made it their mission to destroy the Four Elementals," Lachlan informed us. "They will do everything in their power to stop you from ending the curse."

"What are we supposed to do?" Ariadne questioned.

"You must complete the prophecy," Zara responded. "You must do everything in your power to finish what you have started."

"The Guardians of Aisling will be watching the castle," said Lachlan. "As long as you are here, you will be safe. But the moment each of you steps outside these doors, you will be putting your lives at risk."

"We cannot complete the prophecy from inside the castle," Emery sighed. "We need to go to the towers."

The other Elementals nodded in agreement. The prophecy was destined to be completed in the Four Lone Towers. Although we did not care to venture out into the open, it was impossible to hide behind the castle walls. The fate of Aisling dared to carry us on a perilous journey, and we needed to risk our lives to save the realm.

163

Zara was carefully watching me. She was quite talented at reading my emotions, and she knew exactly what I was thinking. Although she cared for our safety, the headmistress would need to place her trust in our hands.

"At dawn, we will make our way to each of the Four Lone Towers... alone," I announced.

CHAPTER TWENTY-FIVE

The next morning arrived with a sudden start, as I awoke to my sister's icy hand upon my cheek. My eyes opened to greet her pale face and anxious blue gaze. An eerie silence hung in the air, like a heavy chandelier in the house of a nobleman. The morning dew soaked against the castle windows, reflecting the faint light of day.

"It's almost dawn," Emery whispered. "We really must leave."

She opened our stained-glass window to reveal the early morning sky. Streaks of pink and blue lined the horizon as the sun rose gently above the trees. Anticipation had formed a knot in the center of my stomach, but I allowed my mind to focus on the beauty of the sunrise.

There was a moment of silence as we entered the hallway. Each of our eyes stared blankly into the faces of Violet, Kade, and Ronan. Our minds were clouded with countless wistful dreams, although nothing had prepared us for the terrible moments we were destined to brave.

"What are you doing here?" I inquired.

"We know about the prophecy," Ronan responded.

"Zara told us about it," Violet confirmed.

"What are you talking about?" I raised my voice slightly. "Zara wanted to keep this a secret."

Nobody responded as Kade looked me in the eyes. Her wings trembled as a reflective tear dropped from her face. She gathered me into her arms, unable to contain the flood of emotions that brimmed her broken spirit.

"This is important," Kade spoke to me in a whisper. "Even if you don't care to admit it."

The girl's voice was overwhelmed with sorrow as the sleeve of my shirt was soaked in tears. The others watched with sympathetic expressions. After a few moments, I realized that I was fortunate to have such a remarkable group of friends.

"I'm so sorry," Kade whispered as she released me from the embrace. "I never should have held such a terrible grudge."

Her deep blue eyes were tinted the color of strawberries as she continued to wipe the tears away from her skin. Her freckled face held a frightening expression of remorse.

"You are not the only one who should be apologizing," I responded, allowing my gaze to wander across the floor. "It was perfectly rational for you to think we had forgotten about you. I should have told you that we were leaving."

Ronan's eyes appeared almost identical to those of his sister; however, not a single tear ran down his cheeks. His anxious laughter hid something strange beneath its core, and his eyes held a glimmer of worry. My friends watched me for a moment before each of us gathered into a lofty group hug.

❧❧❧

Parting with my loyal companions left my mind in a state of shock. The four of us continued down the passageway and over to the giant stairwell. It was difficult to believe that many of the students were now asleep. Although the castle was silent, my heart was beating loud.

As we reached the blue carpet that rested on the floor of the entrance hall, a voice came from outside the castle. The morning light flooded across the room as we pulled open the doors. Zara and Lachlan were waiting on the castle steps. After the guardian cleared his throat, the headmistress turned to look at us.

For a long moment, no one spoke. I gazed upon the panoramic landscape that rested before us. At the beginning of the year, I would have assumed nothing was wrong; the meadows were silent, and the Night Oak Forest seemed to be natural in appearance. However, that was a time when I had not known about the prophecy. After months of wandering the forests of Aisling, I was able to recognize that something was very wrong. The sun hung low in the sky, and the surrounding meadows drenched in the typical morning dew, but the air was silent, and the curious songbirds were nowhere to be found.

"Those monsters already know we are here," Lachlan grunted as he scanned the distant tree line.

My eyes followed the Guardian's gaze, settling on the deserted border of the dark woodland. It suddenly occurred to me that I had never even seen one of the Creatures of the Night Oak Forest.

"Where are they?" I asked.

"We don't know," Zara explained.

My eyes widened slightly before glancing at the other Elementals. Juniper and Ariadne did not seem startled, but my sister looked back at me with an expression of horror.

"What do you mean?" Emery questioned.

"The Creatures of the Night Oak Forest are invisible," Juniper explained. "This is merely one of the things that make them so frightening."

"I suggest you listen carefully," Ariadne interrupted. "You may not be able to see them coming, but you can hear them if you listen."

"Is this a joke?" I coughed, allowing the words to slip from my mouth with a shiver of disbelief.

Ariadne and Juniper watched us, as if they were surprised we hadn't known. We would soon be facing an invisible monster. Fear and energy mixed within me, until they were muddled to the point of no return.

"All four of you must split up," said Zara.

I nodded silently as my friends exchanged several wary glances. The headmistress was trying to help as much as she could. But there was not another person in all of Aisling who understood the prophecy more than us.

"Run and don't ever look back," Zara whispered.

"If we are going to save the forest, each of us will need to be alive." Ariadne nodded.

"But how will we know if we are being followed?" Emery questioned.

"Trust me," Juniper responded. "You will know."

We each exchanged a nod before gathering into a circle. These girls were my best friends. The thought had occurred to me that I might never see them again, although I forced my mind to shake it away. If we wanted to reach the Four Lone Towers, we needed to believe in ourselves.

One cannot expect to travel far without faith.

As I felt an extra hand rest on my arm, I lifted my head from where it was buried in my sister's shoulder. For the first time in forever, I looked into Zara's eyes and noticed a trace of fear. Hidden beneath the concern was another emotion, which I had learned to recognize as love.

"Lachlan will be keeping a look out for each of you," Zara reminded us. "He has the eyes of a sniper, so don't be afraid to send out a signal for help."

I nodded as the Four Elementals turned to face each other. The presence of my friends gave my heart increased bravery, but I was destined to fight the battle alone. My spirit needed strength.

"The creatures will step inside your head," Ariadne spoke with disgust.

I felt the heat rising from my palms. The Creatures of the Night Oak Forest may have been invisible, but so were the doubt and uncertainty they brought to the human mind. There were times when the unseen could be even more dangerous than what our eyes beheld.

As we separated, my sister glanced back at me. Her pale eyes bore through my skin, as though she wanted to make a promise that we would speak again. Her cream-colored locks rested gently upon her shoulders as the sweet smell of dew-laden grass overwhelmed my senses. A sudden breeze blew through my flaming hair, and my gaze tore away from Emery like the hair-pulling rip of a bandage.

CHAPTER TWENTY-SIX

There was a certain essence about that morning, which was written throughout my memory. As I hurried down the old dirt path, the silence was unbroken. The only sound was the steady rhythm of my heartbeat. Every breath seemed to catch in my chest, as though it did not dare to make a sound.

The sky was illuminated in an extraordinary patchwork of pink and gold. The day did not feel as daunting as I had imagined, although I knew such an emotion would not last for long. As I expected, this state of euphoria was only short-lived.

I heard the sudden crack of a branch and glanced over my shoulder. Something was moving amongst the rosebushes near the end of the path. Although I did not catch sight of the figure, it wasn't difficult to assume its identity. The gardener did not move with such confident steps.

I suppose it was fear that drove my feet forward, as they carried me faster than I had ever gone before. I skidded around a corner of the castle wall. Lachlan had created a strategy that instructed me to take a longer route. He feared the Creatures of the Night Oak Forest planned to target me before the other girls. The headmistress believed a different path might throw them off. As the footsteps of the invisible beast drew close to my heels, my mind was beginning to have second thoughts.

My pursuer was gaining on me.

My ribs were beginning to cramp, as I did not have much practice in long-distance running. However, regardless of the pain, I pushed myself forward. My eyes spotted the courtyard in the distance, and my heart lifted with the knowledge that we were drawing closer to my tower. Perhaps it truly was the fear that had given me this short-lived adrenaline rush, but it was not long before my thoughts pulled me to a halt.

Lachlan stood beside the courtyard gate as he scanned the forest border in the distance. With one shot of the Guardian's arrow, the Creature would be dead. It was a simple end to a dark battle. Even so, I could not allow this to happen, as the Four Elementals were destined to vanquish the Creatures of the Night Oak Forest.

The hot breath of the invisible Creature warmed the back of my neck, sending a terrible shiver down the surface of my spine. Its voice whispered in a familiar, yet distorted tone, *"Silly girl... so inexperienced... so naive."*

I shook my head in an attempt to rid my mind of the poisonous words, but every letter had caught on me like the branches of a thorn bush. Why did the voice concern me? Perhaps there was a part of me that was worried it spoke the truth.

"You don't know what you are doing, Alice!"

My spirit seemed to be standing on the edge of an endless void. The invisible creature was standing at my back. If it dared to push me forward, my fate would fall into the depths of oblivion. I would not allow anyone to have such control over me. Regardless of the words this ghostly demon had dared to whisper, my heart refused to give up.

"You're wrong," I whispered, before turning around to face the monster.

The Creature may have been invisible, but I knew exactly where it stood. The space in front of me was nothing more than gloomy and out of place amongst the peaceful morning air. The atmosphere lacked a quality I had never noticed before.

A ghostly figure appeared from the eerie cloud of fog. The spirit was clothed in a tattered scarlet dress. Her faded skin seemed translucent in the morning sunlight. I gasped with surprise, for her amber eyes were merely a reflection of my own.

After a long moment, I began to realize the truth. The creatures that whisper in our ears are nothing more than the doubts and uncertainties that burrow within our minds. My spirit was stung by the Creature's words, as they mimicked the terrible judgement that rested in the corners of my mind. I allowed these thoughts to poison my soul and tear at my gentle heart.

I glanced over my shoulder, noticing Lachlan was gone. I was alone; however, I was not afraid. The pale reflection was beginning to grow brighter, removing the heavy weight from my chest. Nothing stood in my way.

I was not a terrible beast.

I was Gifted.

As I stared into the reflection of my shining eyes, the strange creature faded away. A beautiful spirit smiled back at me before she began to dissipate into the foggy air. The murkiness evaporated, and the realm of Aisling returned to an iridescent sea of enchantment.

CHAPTER TWENTY-SEVEN

My left hand glided smoothly along the banister as I hurried swiftly up the spiral stairwell. A smile shone brightly from my face as flames danced wildly in my right hand. I leaped through several beams of sunlight, which poured through the tower windows like raw honey from a broken comb. The old stone tower was just as magnificent as the first time I had stepped through its doorway.

I almost expected there to be another obstacle standing in my way. However, when I finally reached the top of the stairwell, the air was peculiarly silent. I held my hand out to grasp the doorknob, but my actions were stopped by a firm prod at my right leg.

I glanced down to see a small gathering of droplet faeries standing cheerfully beside my toes. From where I stood, several feet above them, their voices came to me in the faintest of whispers. I knew they were celebrating, for their smiles seemed to sparkle as their feet danced gracefully beneath them.

The top of the tower was still as my feet carried me through the entrance and toward the balcony. The fog had lifted from the surface of the meadow. In the distance, the other Elementals stood inside their own towers. Their expressions were unreadable from this far away, yet their actions seemed to communicate their knowledge of the task.

A strange feeling stirred in the depths of my heart, awakening from a long and deep slumber. A sudden gust of wind arrived from the mountains of the North, swirling around the stone tower that belonged to Ariadne Moss. The trees of the forest moved through the soil, pulling their roots from the restrains of the earth. They danced with the flowers that bloomed in the dirt, waving their branches toward the countenance of Juniper Stone. The world began to break through the piercing shadows, which had been difficult for many people to discern. Scattered clouds of fresh rain soared across the blue sky, landing on the outstretched hands of my twin sister. The realm of Aisling was beginning to heal from the curse that had lasted more than a lifetime.

But the prophecy was not complete.

It required a selfless deed from my own spirit, although I was not quite sure of the proper act to perform. My Gift was hiding inside a dark cage, waiting for the proper moment to break free. As I searched for the precious key, an unusual whisper came from behind me.

The tower was filled with a thousand shining embers, which drifted slowly throughout the air. Each of them formed into their own shapes and constellations, as they soared closer to each other with freedom. The glowing cinders danced across the room, while I caught sight of the glimmering figure that had formed in the midst of the flames. She took no notice of my presence as her ember skirt twirled in the breeze, and her arms extended gracefully as she danced across the room.

I watched for a moment, as if all my life had been lived in a dream. The realization came flooding in like the sudden shock of diving into a pool of frozen water. This girl made of embers was another reflection of my soul. Unlike the dark and gloomy Alice, who stood before me at the courtyard gate, this figure was a true reflection of my spirit. I was finally beginning to see myself in all of the wonders my Gift had given me.

ACKNOWLEDGMENTS

This book is a work of art. After editing with the unrealistic idea of perfection in mind, I had forgotten the beauty of human flaws. In the words of my father, "People don't want to read something that is perfect, they want to read something that is real."

There will always be sources of discouragement in life; however, you must always remember to believe in yourself more than you believe in the negativity of others. I would like to thank my parents and my entire family for their love, encouragement, and unrivaled advice. This novel is dedicated to all of those who encouraged me along my writing journey.

LETTER FROM THE AUTHOR

This book was the beginning of my career in the world of fiction. It began with a simple idea, which swiftly transformed in the world of my imagination. When I was a young teenager, the fiction section of the bookstore was flooded with depressing and negative stories. The dream of writing my own novel seemed like a fantasy; however, it eventually formed into my extraordinary reality.

Although it involved a ton of hard work and dedication, this story has changed my life for the better. I will always be grateful for the countless letters I have received from my incredible readers. Your love for the realm of Aisling has inspired me to continue the story of the Hanley sisters.

Keep reading!

Sincerely,
Erin Forbes

ABOUT THE AUTHOR

Erin Forbes is a young author who discovered her passion for literature at a very early age. She is known for her vivid descriptions and fantastical fiction. When Erin is not writing, she enjoys art, music, dancing, reading, and riding her horse. She lives on a farm in upstate New York.

37815789R00116

Made in the USA
Middletown, DE
05 March 2019